ONCE UPON A REAL GOOD TIME

LAUREN BLAKELY

Copyright © 2018 by Lauren Blakely
LaurenBlakely.com
Cover Design by © Helen Williams
First Edition Book

All rights reserved. Without limiting the rights under copyright reserved above, no part of this publication may be reproduced, stored in or introduced into a retrieval system, or transmitted, in any form, or by any means (electronic, mechanical, photocopying, recording, or otherwise) without the prior written permission of both the copyright owner and the above publisher of this book.

This is a work of fiction. Names, characters, places, brands, media, and incidents are either the product of the author's imagination or are used fictitiously. The author acknowledges the trademarked status and trademark owners of various products referenced in this work of fiction, which have been used without permission. The publication/use of these trademarks is not authorized, associated with, or sponsored by the trademark owners. This ebook is licensed for your personal use only. This ebook may not be re-sold or given away to other people. If you would like to share this book with another person, please purchase an additional copy for each person you share it with. If you are reading this book and did not purchase it, or it was not purchased for your use only, then you should return it and purchase your own copy. Thank you for respecting the author's work.

ALSO BY LAUREN BLAKELY

Big Rock Series

Big Rock

Mister O

Well Hung

Full Package

Joy Ride

Hard Wood

One Love Series dual-POV Standalones

The Sexy One

The Only One

The Hot One

Standalones

The Knocked Up Plan

Most Valuable Playboy

Stud Finder

The V Card

Most Likely to Score

Wanderlust

Come As You Are

Part-Time Lover

The Real Deal

Unbreak My Heart

Once Upon a Real Good Time

Once Upon a Sure Thing

Once Upon a Wild Fling

Unzipped (Fall 2018)

Far Too Tempting

21 Stolen Kisses

Playing With Her Heart

Out of Bounds

The Caught Up in Love Series
Caught Up In Us

Pretending He's Mine

Trophy Husband

Stars in Their Eyes

The No Regrets Series
The Thrill of It

The Start of Us

Every Second With You

The Seductive Nights Series

First Night (Julia and Clay, prequel novella)

Night After Night (Julia and Clay, book one)

After This Night (Julia and Clay, book two)

One More Night (Julia and Clay, book three)

A Wildly Seductive Night (Julia and Clay novella, book 3.5)

The Joy Delivered Duet

Nights With Him (A standalone novel about Michelle and Jack)

Forbidden Nights (A standalone novel about Nate and Casey)

The Sinful Nights Series

Sweet Sinful Nights

Sinful Desire

Sinful Longing

Sinful Love

The Fighting Fire Series

Burn For Me (Smith and Jamie)

Melt for Him (Megan and Becker)

Consumed By You (Travis and Cara)

The Jewel Series

A two-book sexy contemporary romance series

The Sapphire Affair

The Sapphire Heist

ABOUT

That smoking hot one-night stand with a former rock star?

Turns out he's my son's new music teacher. Oops.

But I didn't know that the night I met Campbell. All I knew was he played my body the same way he played a guitar — like he owned it.

My libido is still high-fiving me after being self-served for too many years, and we're both ready for another night or two of fun, especially since we don't just have chemistry in bed — we connect over everything.

That is, until I learn he's the man who'll be coming to my house twice a week to teach my son — the best music lessons money can buy.

Time to turn down the volume on our shenanigans. Only that's easier said than done.

***

I can rock a guitar solo in front of thousands, I can write chart-topping tunes, and I can absolutely stop thinking about my student's mother naked.

After all, I'm a single parent too, and I know what it's like to put your kid first. That's what I do every damn day.

Trouble is, now that I've had Mackenzie, it's hard — and I do mean hard — to stop wanting her. Harder too when I get to know her, and learn she's an awesome mom, a great friend, and, oh yeah, she happens to get along perfectly with my daughter.

All we have to do is set some rules. No dating, no nookie when the kids are around, and no one gets hurt.

It's all working out beautifully. Until we start breaking the rules, one by one.

Making music with her in the bedroom is easy. But will we be more than just a real good time when the music stops?

CHAPTER 1

Mackenzie

I'm not checking him out.

I am solely focused on answering the next trivia question. The game emcee spouts it out for the four teams vying for the prize at The Grouchy Owl bar. The prize being bragging rights.

The hostess clears her throat, brings the mic to her mouth, and asks the question: "Which Las Vegas hotel did the bachelor party stay at—"

I'm perched forward in the chair whispering the answer to my teammate—*Caesars, Caesars, Caesars*—so we can write it on the answer slip before the hostess even finishes.

"—in the 2009 movie *The Hangover*?"

"So easy," I say to Roxy as she smacks my palm and mouths *ringer* while filling in the answer.

I'm not a ringer.

I was simply fed a steady diet of Trivial Pursuit, trivia books, and endless facts about the world as a kid.

That's all.

Also, I love trivia. Trivia helped me through some tough times as an adult, and by tough, I mean anxiety-ridden, sleepless, and stressful. That kind of tough.

As the hostess flips her cards to the next question, the guy on stage—the one I'm not at all checking out—adjusts the amp for his guitar. The Grouchy Owl has a little bit of everything—from darts, to pub quizzes, to pool, to live music from local bands. It's like a Vegas hotel right here in the West Village. Big Ike doesn't want patrons to leave, so she makes sure the entertainment options are plentiful.

And if that handsome hottie stays on the stage, I won't want to head home for a long, long time. Except I'll have to. I'm Cinderella, and I turn into a pumpkin in minutes.

But for now ... *Hello, nice view.*

As the guy turns the knob on the amp, his brown hair flops over his eyes. He flicks it off his forehead with a quick snap then runs his fingers down the strings on his guitar. Those fingers fly.

I bet they'd fly other places too.

Come to think of it, I better give him a full and proper appraisal, especially since the *Jeopardy!*-style theme clock blasting from the hostess's phone is counting down the seconds till we've all penned an answer to her latest question, which means I have time to ogle.

A thin blue T-shirt reveals inked and toned arms, and stubble covers his jaw—deliberate stubble. Not the I-didn't-shave-today stubble, but a healthy amount of scruff. Yum.

"Would you like your camera to take a picture, or have you captured Guitar Hero in your brain for posterity?"

I jerk my gaze back to Roxy.

Note to self: develop some subtlety when ogling. Especially since you're out of practice on . . . everything.

I flip a strand of hair off my shoulder. "I wasn't checking him out."

Roxy rolls her hazel eyes. "I'm hereby awarding you a trophy for the most unconvincing attempt at denial ever."

I huff. "Fine. He's crazy handsome. Look at those cheekbones. Those lips. Those eyes."

She sings his praises too. "Those hands, that ass, those legs."

I swat her arm. "Stop perving on my eye candy."

My best friend smiles wickedly. "It's so easy to see through you."

"I didn't deny it for long." I hold up one finger. "For, like, one round of denial."

She reaches for my iced tea and hands it to me. "Speaking of rounds, take a drink. It'll make you strong for the final round of the game."

"Sometimes I think you use me for the useless facts in my head."

"You don't have to think it. You know I do."

"Love you too."

"Also," she says, leaning closer, "your eye candy was checking you out as well."

My eyebrows shoot into my hairline. "Lying liar who lies."

The hostess taps the mic from her spot in front of Mr. Guitar Hero. "And now, for the final question in The Tuesday Night Grouchy Owl Pub Quiz . . ."

Like synchronized swimmers, Roxy and I straighten our shoulders in unison. I grab the pencil. Hold it tight. This isn't a first-to-the-bell game, but there's something about being on high alert that feels right. I'm ready.

Questions zip through my brain, answers following instantly as my mind exercises itself. *The Beatles were first the Quarrymen; at sixty-three, Jupiter has the most moons; the Pacific is 8,000 meters deep.*

"Which Whitney Houston song is an anagram of 'mention mine to me'?"

What the what?

I turn to Roxy, and we are matching slack-jawed, WTH memes. Admittedly, pop music is my weakest category, but I can handle the basic questions surrounding the genre. This question is a little left of center though. I try my best to cycle through the diva's tunes. We mouth to each other the big Whitney hits: "I Will Always Love You." "Greatest Love of All." "How Will I Know."

I shake my head, and Roxy furrows her brow.

I stare off at the stage when the guy with the surfer hair catches my gaze and mouths *hi*, startling me. Is he talking to me? Oh yes, he is, since he follows that *hi* with four more words.

Holy smokes.

He slipped me the answer.

I'm officially in love.

I grab Roxy's arm. "'One Moment in Time,'" I whisper, and I unleash a smile at Guitar Hero. Because we're one step closer to winning, and that's one of my favorite things to do on a Tuesday night during my hour-long escape at The Grouchy Owl.

But wait. How does hottie know a Whitney Houston song? Straight men can know Whitney tunes, right?

Of course they can. God, I hope so. He looks seriously straight. He's staring at me like a man who enjoys boobs stares at a woman who has them.

I sneak another peek. His fingers slide down the guitar as he tunes it. He raises an eyebrow and locks eyes with me, his lips curving up.

My stupid stomach has the audacity to swoop.

Of course, in my stomach's defense, the loop-de-loop makes complete sense. Not only is he a babe registering easily at 15.5 on the only-goes-to-ten babe-o-meter, but he's holding a guitar. The way he wields the Stratocaster cranks my libido up high.

That might be due to said libido's sadly solo life these days.

As the hostess collects the answer slips, Roxy nudges my shoulder. "Go talk to him."

I roll my eyes.

"Oh please. You can do it," she adds.

"I'm not going to go talk to some random guy onstage at a bar, prepping for his set."

"Why not?"

"Because," I sputter. "Because it's dangerous, risky, crazy, and I have a thirteen-year-old at home."

"Isn't Kyle out right now? Practice or something?"

"Yes, but I need to pick him up in a few minutes, and that means I should go."

Roxy pouts. "Don't go before we find out if we win. And don't go before you talk to Mr. Steamy McMusic."

I laugh and shake my head. "You go talk to him."

"I can't. He has your eye marks all over him."

"Good. I own the view."

I stand, and Roxy joins me to give a quick goodbye hug. "Love ya," I say.

"Thanks for coming out to play. It's nice to see your face every now and then."

I head to the door, nearly bumping into the curly-haired Big Ike on the way.

"Hey, Mack. Is Kyle ready for Pine Notes?" she barks.

"Starts tomorrow. He's so excited." As the keeper of all musical knowledge in the tristate area, she recommended the music camp my son's attending starting tomorrow, and it sounds like a fantastic opportunity.

"The teachers there are great. He's going to love it."

I give a thumbs-up, wave goodbye, and don't even bother to check and see if Mr. Guitar Hero is watching me, though I'm tempted.

I head down the street then turn the corner, hoofing it a few blocks to the community center where Kyle practices with some of the other kids his age. He's formed an ad hoc sort of string quartet with some friends in the city who like the same music as he does. Shortly after I arrive, the kids stream outside, and I smile at my little blond-haired, brown-eyed guy.

Okay, he's not so little anymore.

But he's still my guy.

"Hey, monster," I say. "How was practice?"

He slings his violin case over his shoulder. "It was good. We worked on a new Brahms concerto that's totally dope."

"That's the only way Brahms concertos should be."

During the short walk home, Kyle regales me with details of the music. His voice rises as he grows more excited, then he smiles at me, the metal in his braces occupying most of the real estate on his teeth.

We reach our building and go inside.

"Did you win big tonight?" he asks once we're in our apartment.

I shrug and smile. "Don't know. But we fought valiantly. Are you hungry? Want me to cook some scrambled eggs with rosemary country potatoes?"

He pats his flat belly on his trim frame. "I'm still stuffed from the sandwich you made earlier."

I gesture to his room. "Big day tomorrow. Go put your violin away and get ready for bed. We're leaving to take you to camp at seven thirty sharp."

He salutes me on the way to his room.

A few minutes later, Kyle has brushed his teeth, washed his face, and is reading his biography of

Mariano Rivera. I park myself on the edge of his twin bed and knock on the book's spine. "Good guy or bad guy?"

Kyle only reads books about sports stars if he deems them good guys, so I know the answer, but I ask anyway because I like knowing what's in his head. For now, since he hasn't hit puberty with a vengeance, he usually tells me what's on his mind. "Definitely a good guy. He's also the greatest closer of all time."

I'm not even a sports fan, but I know that. "Six hundred fifty career saves isn't too shabby."

"You're such a dork."

"From one to another." I tap his forehead. "Did you take your headache meds?"

He gives me a thumbs-up.

"Good." I give him a kiss and say good night. "Love you so much."

"Love you too, Mom."

When I retreat to my room, I find a message from Roxy on my phone.

Roxy: We won, but it was by the hair of our chinny-chin-chins! It was super close—we need to be tighter next time. Also, all this could be yours.

The screen fills with an image and tingles zip down my body. Damn, that man is dangerously handsome, especially with the intensity in his eyes as he plays that instrument.

I sigh happily. I'm so checking him out.

What's the harm? He's likely in some band that's making a one-night-only appearance at The Grouchy Owl, like many of the bands that play there do. I'll probably never see him again. Unless you count later tonight in my dreams. Because that face and those hands are definitely fodder for a good night fantasy.

Besides, fantasies are the only times I've had any action lately, and by lately, I mean years.

CHAPTER 2

Campbell

I get lost in the music as I play. I lose myself in how notes and chords flow through my veins and pour from my fingers. Playing like this—incognito—makes me feel as if I'm flying high, like I can love performing the same way I did when I was younger.

We cruise through our set of covers and originals. As we do, I keep one eye open, so to speak, for the woman I spotted earlier, hoping she'll slip back inside. I scan the crowd from time to time, searching for those freckles, those pink lips, the tattoo I caught a peek of on her shoulder when her top slouched down.

She disappeared an hour ago, and I haven't seen her since.

When the set is over, my curious eyes search once more for the dirty-blonde who's damn near addicted to trivia games. She was here last week, and we weren't playing then, just meeting with Big Ike, but I have a good memory for inked and brainy women.

At least, I'm guessing she has a solid noggin since I saw the intensity in her eyes and the set of her mouth as she'd worked through the quiz questions.

"Encore, encore!" a leggy brunette near the front shouts, cupping her hands over her mouth.

I turn to my Righteous Surfboards bandmates, asking with my eyes if they're ready. The guys nod, and since we've played all our originals earlier in the night, we dive into a cover of "Wicked Game," since that one seems to please audiences the most. When we're done, I thank the crowd, turn off the mics, then high-five the guys for a good show.

"Dude, that was a most awesome gig," says our bassist, Cade, who's all of twenty-five. He talks like Sean Penn in *Fast Times at Ridgemont High*, and dresses like him too, down to the Vans. I'm pretty sure he's stuck in a time warp.

JJ stuffs his drumsticks in his back jeans pocket and glances at the crowd, dispersing and heading for the bar. He looks to me. "Man, for only our fifth show, that was impressive, but if you'd let us say who you are, we can attract a bigger crowd."

I give my longtime childhood friend a we're-not-going-to-have-this-conversation-again look. JJ knows the score. "But I won't, so we can't."

He mimes holding a knife and driving it into his broad chest. "You're killing me, Campbell. Why don't you take the knife and stab me?"

"Why don't you let the music do its job in bringing the audience?"

"Because, bro, your name. Who you are. That face!"

Cade jumps in. "Yeah, you have a face that the teens and the MILFs both like."

I laugh at our resident young'un as I drag a hand across my chin. "The face has aged many years since the teens liked it. Also, can we *not* talk about teen girls digging me?"

Cade points at me. "Don't try to deny it. When you deny the power of your own face, you're dismissing what the good universe gave you."

But they know the true reason I don't use my *former* stage name, and it has nothing to do with MILFs or tweens. I don't use Mason Hart because that's not the life I'm living now. I want my life to be simpler.

I say goodbye to the guys and head home to my place across town.

This is the life I'm living now.

* * *

When I reach the tenth floor of my Murray Hill apartment, the scent of something sugary and mouth-watering wafts down the hall. I slide the key in the lock of 10B, but the door gives instantly.

The door is yanked open from the other side. Samantha smiles widely. "I have a surprise for you!"

I crinkle my nose, sniffing. "Hmm . . . what is that? Better not be liquor."

My fourteen-year-old rolls her green eyes. No one can roll eyes like a teenage girl.

"Dad," she chides.

Nor chide as well.

"Well, what is that smell?"

"It's vanilla. I'm baking." She shakes her head. "You're so ridiculous."

"Okay. It smells good." I drop my guitar case by the door and give her a peck on the forehead.

"Also, how can you even say that? Do you think the chocolate chip-stuffed soft pretzels smell like liquor?"

My stomach growls, answering for us both. "Clearly, my stomach and I think they smell wonderful. But I'm obligated to ask if there's any liquor in the house that I don't know about."

"Obligated by whom?"

I flap my arms around. "By the code of..."

"Code of nosy dads?"

"I'm not nosy."

I'm so nosy.

She ushers me into the open-space, state-of-the-art kitchen. She asked for an upgrade, and I did it, because seriously, how am I supposed to deny a kid who doesn't have an ounce of trouble in her body?

At least, none I'm aware of yet.

She opens the oven and grabs a tray from it. Her looped-over blonde hair falls against her cheek, and she bats it away with a pink skull-and-crossbones oven mitt, complete with bows daintily tied on the skull heads. Irony, thy name is Samantha Evans.

"When I was trying to decide what to bake, I asked myself what great tastes go great together," she says as I inhale the warm, homey scent. "And the answer is pretzels and cookies. I devised this recipe for chocolate chip cookie pretzels—basically, the cookie is stuffed *inside* the pretzel. I call them cookie-etzels, and I think they're legitimately the best thing ever, but they might also be the worst thing anyone has ever tasted."

Everything is both the best and the worst at the same time for her.

There is no in-between.

She shoves a cookie pretzel at me, bouncing on

her Adidas-clad feet. I take the treat, pop it in my mouth, and fall in love with a cookie-etzel.

This kid has mad baking skills.

"It's delicious," I declare as she adjusts her apron.

She narrows her eyes, skeptical to the end. "You're not just saying that?" The excitement in her tone says she wants to believe me.

"Would I lie to you?"

She parks her hands on her hips. "You one hundred percent would."

Laughing, I answer her, "Then why do you ask me to test your stuff?"

"Because you're here."

I wave at the door. "So is Dave the doorman. Go ask him."

"Good idea. Come with me?"

I shake my head. "Nope. You've lived here for five years. You know him. Go give him one and ask his opinion."

She grabs a plate and says she'll be right back.

She scurries downstairs as I ready myself for bed, yawning while I brush my teeth. These late-night gigs are fun, but they were a helluva lot easier when I was seventeen. I head to the kitchen for a glass of water, downing it quickly.

When Samantha returns, she gives me a thumbs-up. "He said I should open a corner bakery, and there would be a line down the street every day."

"I told you so."

"Maybe I'll believe you. Maybe I won't." She shrugs happily. "Also, can you, you know, go?" This last request comes out moderately sheepishly.

I narrow my eyes. "Go where? I live here. I just returned home."

She shoos me out of the kitchen. "To your room, Dad. I need to record a video now for my cooking show on these cookie-etzels, and I can't have you in it."

"You wouldn't want anyone on Instagram to know you have a dad."

"Obviously."

That's the thing—I'm unwelcome in her videos because I'm her father, not because I was once Mason Hart, one-third of the band of brothers once known as the Heartbreakers.

But that's fine with me.

This is my life. My fourteen-year-old has sent me to my room.

I wouldn't have it any other way.

CHAPTER 3

Mackenzie

Two weeks later

When I was younger and living in the wilds of Connecticut, I used to ride my bike everywhere. To and from school. Around the neighborhood. With my sister, Jackie, to the convenience store to grab Butterfingers and Skittles after school.

Now I am one of the many in Manhattan who ride to nowhere in a mirrored room. Spin class is a thoroughly modern form of torture up there with eyebrow threading and bikini waxing. But that's okay, because I'm really riding somewhere.

"Five more minutes. Climb the hill. Give it one last push. You can do it."

The instructor in the class that Jamison and I attend is peppy and full of energy, but if she wasn't, her card as an exercise instructor would be instantly revoked by the Committee of Cheery Exercise Instructors. That governing body ensures that anyone leading a class at a gym or fitness center must possess the personality of a second-grade teacher on caffeine. Or a puppy. Ideally, both combined into one compact, trim, toned, muscular figure.

Which Candace possesses.

And honestly, which I can claim now too—the toned figure, that is—thanks to this class. Even though I'm here to train for an upcoming Spin for Kids fundraiser to benefit leukemia, I started spin classes last year when I finally decided I wanted to take better charge of my health.

Fifteen pounds have evaporated off me, and I feel better and healthier. It hasn't changed my fortunes when it comes to dating though, but that's probably more related to the little fact that I DON'T HAVE TIME TO DATE.

"All right, girl," Jamison whispers to me from the bike next to mine. He's in town for a bit between *Hello, Dolly!* and a new production of *Chicago*. "It's your last night of freedom. Are you going to party hard or do online Scrabble?"

As sweat trickles down my neck, I give my son's father a sneer and pant out the answer. "No. I'm going to go really crazy and finally watch that Idris Elba movie I've been wanting to see."

"Ooh, that man is such a fine specimen."

So was the guy at The Grouchy Owl.

Jamison cycles harder. He loves to be the best in the class. His body shows it—he's in flick-a-quarter-off-him shape. I'm jealous, but only slightly, because he works out at five most mornings when he's on the road, and that sounds like a worse way to spend an hour than bikini waxing.

As I pedal harder up a hill that's as vicious as Candace promised, I manage to answer between breaths. "I'm probably going to review some of my top trivia questions tonight. We won two weeks ago, but it was too close for comfort, so I need to shore up my knowledge."

Jamison's goatee-lined jaw drops as if he's completely shocked. "Was there some tall, handsome brainiac who distracted you?"

I snort and stare hard at a fascinating mark on the wall. That paint speck is mesmerizing, and how on earth could Jamison tell?

"I wish," I say as we crest the hill. If I tell him I was admiring the guitarist's assets, he'll ask a bajillion questions, find out the guitarist's name, track him down on social media, and ask him to go out with me.

Jamison is a meddler. He's so good at it that I'm

pretty sure he invented meddling.

"You did it! Now it's time to cool down," Candace shouts, thrusting her arms in the air.

I breathe fifty million sighs of relief that the rest of the class is downhill.

"Back to your last night of freedom, missy," Jamison says, returning without losing a beat to his efforts to agent, manage, and event plan my social life. "You need to do something fun before Kyle comes back tomorrow."

I arch an unthreaded brow as I slow my pedaling. "I do?"

"Yes. You." He nods. *Vigorously.* It's the only way Jamison can nod.

"Why do I need to do something fun?" I love to egg him on.

He rolls his big brown eyes. "Because it's return to Mommyville tomorrow. You never do anything but be his mom."

"Because I *am* his mom."

"You're wasting your youth as a martyr, you know."

"No, I'm giving him stability, you manwhore."

He pretends to look shocked. "How can you say that about *moi*?"

I laugh. "Because it's true."

"I mean, besides that," he says, with a wink. His expression turns serious, his tone concerned. "But,

Mack, I want to see you out and having fun. I know a lot has fallen on your shoulders with my travel schedule, and you bore the brunt of Kyle's headache management."

Truer words were never spoken. Our kid suffered through wicked migraines in grade school, the kind that left him curled up in a fetal position in a pitch-black room. We scoured all the online med boards, tested every combination of food, recorded details in countless headache diaries, and tried endless over-the-counter meds until we finally found a doc who *got* it and prescribed the right preventative meds for him. Those daily pills are life-changing. In fact, once he started them, his violin skills shot to the stratosphere. He was not only learning, but mastering concertos in no time. His teacher has told us he's more talented than she is now, which is one of those things a teacher says that makes you scratch your head, rub your ear, and figure you're hearing things.

Jamison continues making his case. "Now that he's doing better and kicking butt with violin and everything, why don't you try to go out more?"

"I do trivia nights," I point out, because that's more than enough for me. After an unexpected pregnancy and all the changes that rippled through my life because of it, I've still managed to make Kyle my number one priority *and* build a business that supports my kid and me. That doesn't give me much time for more than trivia nights, but I love trivia, so that's fine by me.

He sighs dramatically. "Besides trivia. I mean dating. You know that thing two people do when they like each other?"

I adopt an ultra-confused look. "I don't know what that is."

"That's my point! It's a sin you're not going out more. You are young and, evidently, attractive to men."

I give him a you've-got-to-be-kidding-me look.

"Fine, you're attractive empirically. But the clock is ticking."

"I'm young. I'm only thirty-three."

"You turn thirty-four in a month."

I hiss at him. "Thirty-four is still young, and I can date when he's safely at college. Besides, I'm kind of crazy excited to see him tomorrow and hear how camp was. Aren't you?"

"Yes, Mack. I'm crazy excited to see him too. I already have the rental car booked, and I think the new year is going to be a good one with all the opportunities at the community center—playing space, and concerts, and practice rooms for his string quartet. But have you thought that maybe instead of spending the night with Idris Elba, you could, I don't know, go crazy and do something besides play trivia games?"

I stick out my tongue at him. "Why?"

"You're such a good girl. You need fun."

I chuckle privately. If he saw my internet history, he wouldn't think I was a good girl. Tumblr knows the real me and knows to never be in safe mode after ten p.m.

Jamison goes quiet for a second as our pedaling slows further. Jamison is rarely quiet. If he's quiet, he's thinking, and when he's thinking, he's stirring things up. He wiggles his eyebrows and, like he's luring a dog with a toy, says, "Fun might make you a better mom, and studies show moms who let themselves have a little fun now and then are better at parenting."

I narrow my eyes. "You're playing dirty."

He smirks. "I always play dirty."

A chipper voice carries across the room. "Well done, class. Well done! We're getting ready for our fundraiser. Keep it up!" Candace beams from the front of the class.

At last, I dismount, and my legs are jelly. My muscles scream at me. They ask why I make them suffer in this class. But I make them suffer because it's good for them and for the kids we're raising money for.

I grab my water bottle, and Jamison and I leave the spin room, moving our your-love-life-resembles-a-cobweb lecture to the hallway.

"Look, I know you're busy. I know you're the most in-demand graphic designer in the history of all the universes, but especially in this universe of New York City, which I wish I spent more time in." Jamison works as a theater producer, overseeing a handful of touring productions, which means he's on the road frequently. "But I worry about you. I want you to embrace the YOLO."

"Are you fourteen?"

A nod. "In some ways. You need to live it up. Life is short, make the most of it. You'll be glad you did, and you'll be like this beautiful, recharged woman who excels at momming even more than she does now."

"Momming isn't a word."

"Now it is."

"If I go out tonight, will it get you off my back about going out?"

He laughs. "As if anything would get me off your back. Baby, you're stuck with me."

I stare at him. "I've been stuck with you ever since your crazy idea back in college."

"But it was worth it. Admit it. So worth it."

I'll never regret saying yes to my best friend when he told me in our senior year that he'd never had sex with a girl and was curious if he was missing anything as he explored his bisexuality.

I was his test case, and we learned two things—

I'm a fertile myrtle, and Jamison definitely prefers dudes.

I never thought anything more would come of it than me doing a favor for my bestie—giving him a chance to learn once and for all if he loved dicks 100 percent of the time or only a little more than half. Turned out, one screw with me was enough to both confirm he was 100 percent pro-penis and also to accidentally put a bun in my oven.

He goes on and on about some hip new club I need to check out. I'm sure you have to have ripped jeans or heels four inches high or a resting bitch face the likes of which I've never had to get in. I'm not going to go. But I humor him by listening.

"And they have drinks with names like Shelter and Sin."

Wow, that sounds dreadful. "Perfect for me," I say with a fake smile.

"You're not going, are you?"

"Of course, I'm not. But I'll see you bright and early for the drive to camp."

He shakes his head and sighs dramatically. "What am I supposed to do with you?"

* * *

My evening goes like this: I take a shower, singing show tunes at the top of my lungs. Afterward, I blow-dry my hair, slather on lotion, and take a leisurely stroll through some of my favorite eight-inches-and-more feeds. Hey, when the kid's away, I like to take a few extra solo flights, and I happen to be a big fan of above-average assets on the male form.

Next is a quick game of Words with Friends with one of my fellow designers. I crush it, and then I hop over to Netflix. *The Mountain Between Us* or *Molly's Game*? The debate is real.

As I watch the trailers to decide which mood I'm in, a text message pops up on my phone.

Roxy: Turns out it's game night tonight. Want to go out?

My senses go on high alert.

I pace my small apartment, weighing my options. I could stay home and watch both movies. Hell, I could go full Idris marathon. Or I could read. Stopping in front of my bookshelf, I run my thumb over the new trivia book my dad sent me, stuffed with fun facts about modern geography. It's totally addictive.

On the other hand ...

Jamison's words ring loud in my ears. Do I need fun instead? Is fun another trivia night? Or is fun the movie marathon and a new book?

Before I arrive at an answer, a second message lands on the screen.

Roxy: Also, Hendrix is here.

Mackenzie: Hendrix?

Roxy: The guitar hottie!!!

Ohhhhhhhhh.
Well.
That does sound precisely like fun.
Fine, fine. Nothing is going to happen with the guitar hottie, but I like looking at eye candy.
Eye candy equals my kind of fun.
I pull on my skinny jeans—thank you, spin class, for the way the denim hugs and loves my ass and thighs—tug on a top that slouches off one shoulder, and slide into heels.
I consider my reflection in the mirror as I comb on mascara and slick on pink lip gloss. Big brown eyes, dark-blonde hair, cute freckles, and sexy hummingbird ink on my shoulder, inspired by my favorite Pablo Neruda quote. *The hummingbird in*

flight is a water-spark, an incandescent drip of American fire.

I give myself a thumbs-up, then a talking-to. "You are fun, Mackenzie. You are so fun you're like the living, breathing definition of fun."

I head to The Grouchy Owl.

Maybe it's not exactly what Jamison had in mind. But who cares as long as it's game night with an added benefit of a nice view?

When I walk into the bar, I don't spot the usual signs for game night. But I do see a tall, toned man with dark floppy hair, a fine ass, and ripped jeans as he walks down the hall toward the back of the bar.

Roxy did not lie.

A shiver runs through me, and I stare till he turns the corner.

Hot damn.

I find Roxy at the bar. "Hey, you. Where's the game night crew?" I survey the scene, but I don't spot the usual emcee or the other regular teams. I don't even see Big Ike here tonight.

Roxy wiggles her eyebrows. "It's not game night. Guitar Hero's band is playing. You're welcome."

I smack her arm. "Are you in cahoots with Jamison?"

She laughs. "Mackenzie, I'm in cahoots with your libido. It called me up and told me a good friend would help you get laid."

"How do you know Guitar Hero wants that?"

"I saw the way he looked at you. I'm not blind. Now, let's go enjoy some pop music. Sorry it's not *Hamilton*, but hopefully you can find it in you to enjoy it."

"I'll do my best."

I do better than my best, because when the object of my dirty daydreams walks over to his guitar, my libido definitely sits up and takes notice.

More like stands and nearly rushes the stage.

He's hotter than I remembered, and if he were an ice cream cone, I'd order a triple scoop and lick him up.

His eyes scan the crowd. A charge runs down my spine as I remember him mouthing the clue to me the other week, and again as I imagine other things his mouth might do.

As his eyes find me, that charge turns to full-blown electricity. His gaze locks with mine, and when it does, a lopsided grin spreads on his handsome face.

Oh my.

Maybe it is time to focus on me tonight. Maybe it is time to have some fun. One night of wild abandon sounds perfectly reasonable. In fact, I think my libido is in cahoots with me, and I have a feeling we both might win.

CHAPTER 4

Campbell

An hour on stage here and there in a dimly lit bar is enough for me these days.

That's why I don't worry too much about whether the audience is big or small, male or female, packed or not packed. I play because, well, I have to.

But tonight? I'm playing for a woman. Because she's back.

The trivia queen has returned, and she's dancing to our tunes. Man, there's nothing hotter than a hot woman dancing to a song you wrote, a song you're singing.

The Righteous Surfboards are a little bit of pop, a

little bit of rock, a little bit of indie flare, and plenty of guitar. *Always guitar.*

The blonde with the constellation of freckles shakes her hips near the front of the stage, thanks to her friend who tugged her out to the dance floor.

God bless women's friends. If women didn't have friends, they might not ever talk to us. But I love wingwomen who push their friends to dance.

I'm playing for the trivia queen. I'm singing for her. I don't even know her name. I don't care. When I look at her, something crackles—an energy, a spark.

When I finish the song, I bend closer to the mic stand. "Thank you very much. And for our last number, any requests?"

The redhead next to my front-row dancer nudges her. She shakes her head, and her friend mouths *c'mon*, then the blonde shouts, "'One Moment in Time' by Whitney Houston."

A groan goes up from the guys in the band.

I'm not a huge fan of the diva—nothing against her. She's just not my cup of tea, even though I'm familiar with most big pop songs—but I love that my dancing queen remembers that moment between us a couple weeks ago.

Despite the bellyaching from the band, I won't back down. I have a hell of an ear and can pick up most tunes quickly. I strum a chorus from the song, lean into the mic, and sing the refrain.

The blonde's brown eyes widen in excitement, and she claps her hands in delight.

"Anything else?" I rattle off the names of some popular bands we cover.

A blank look appears on her face for most of them, and then she shouts, "'High Flying Adored.'"

I arch a brow. "*Evita*? You want us to sing *Evita*?"

"Yes!"

Cade groans.

I laugh at him. "My bassist is going to revolt."

She tosses out another. "'One Day More.'"

Everyone loves *Les Mis*. Except for my guys. "Look, we'll only do badass modern musicals. Either *Hamilton* or *Book of Mormon*," Cade says begrudgingly into the mic.

"I love both," the woman shouts.

We launch into "I Believe" from *The Book of Mormon* for a few bars, and when we're done, the woman with the hummingbird tattoo thrusts her arms in the air in victory. Determined to talk to her, I step away from the mic and move to the edge of the stage where I beckon to her.

She points to herself and mouths *me?*

"Yeah, you."

She steps forward a few feet, and her smile is so damn adorable I want to kiss it off.

"Stay. Have a drink with me."

"Really?"

I laugh. "Yeah, really."

She furrows her brow. "Are you sure?"

I laugh again. "I'm positive. Don't go anywhere."

"I'll be over there." She points to the bar.

After we break down the equipment, I pack up my guitar and stow the case in the back room before I head around to the bar. She's with her redheaded friend, who shoves her phone at me, displaying a page from the bar's social media page mentioning our gig.

"I'm Roxy. I presume you're Campbell from the Righteous Surfboards?" The redhead taps on my picture and my extremely short bio. *Campbell lives and breathes music, playing some nights, and teaching music during the day.*

"That's me."

My full given name is Campbell Mason Evans and when my brother and I started the band, we used Mason and Miller Hart. Because . . . *alliteration and hearts*. When our youngest brother, Miles, joined us a few years later, we had triple alliteration working in our favor.

Though the guys in the Righteous Surfboards want me to use Mason Hart on the bar's social media, there's no way I'd get on stage under that name. Yes, the Heartbreakers have made a lot of my life possible. The money from our music has paid for my apartment. It will pay for my daughter's college someday. It funds her private school now, and damn near anything else.

But I don't want to be a Heartbreaker, because I don't want the fame and notoriety that come with it. Or the nights away from home. And tonight, I want to be a regular guy who plays the guitar and happens to have caught the attention of an incredibly sexy woman.

Roxy cups her hand over her friend's shoulder. "Campbell, this is Mackenzie. If you're a dick, I'll find you and use all my Krav Maga skills on you."

I nod crisply. "Duly noted."

"Plus, Big Ike has our backs," Roxy says.

I hold up my hands in surrender. "I'd never cross Big Ike, and I guarantee you won't need to drop-kick me."

Mackenzie wipes her forehead in a dramatic *whew*, then Roxy gives her friend a hug and takes off.

I turn to Mackenzie, glad to have a name to go with the face. The gorgeous face. She's not overly made-up—she wears a hint of makeup and some gloss, but that's about all, as if she knows her strength lies in her natural smile, her freckles, and the twinkle in her milk-chocolate eyes.

I tip my forehead to Roxy. "It's always good to have a friend who's willing to go to war for you."

She flashes a smile. "If situations were reversed, though, I'd be limited to lobbing invectives and barbed words, so I'm glad she's the defender in this case."

"I bet your barbed words pack a sharp punch though."

"Let's hope no one needs to find out."

I nod toward the bartender. "What's your poison?"

"Vodka tonic would be great. But hold the poison."

I laugh. "No arsenic tonight, I promise."

"Or any night, really."

"Arsenic is always off the menu."

She laughs, then it fades as she fiddles with the bracelets on her left hand, like she needs something to do, and I like that she's a little nervous. It shows this isn't her regular kit and caboodle. I had plenty of that when I was playing with the Heartbreakers. I don't need or want it again.

I order her drink and a beer for myself, then turn to the woman I sang to, the very same woman I had my eyes on the first time I spied her at this bar in the Village a few weeks ago. Seeing her tonight feels like luck, or maybe just a chance I need to seize. Samantha is spending the night at a friend's house, and I see no reason why I shouldn't get to know the woman who danced in the audience to my songs.

Danced, and also eye-fucked me.

And I loved every single second of it.

I tap the bar. "Call me crazy, but I have this wild feeling you're a big Broadway fan. Not sure where I got that idea. Just picking up on a vibe," I say playfully.

Her eyes crinkle. "My knowledge of pop music is woefully limited, but I do love me some show tunes, and I'm also all about classical music."

My eyebrows rise. "That's interesting. I don't hear that very often." Well, I do hear that often, but not in this sort of situation.

"Big fan of Brahms, Chopin, Beethoven." She taps her chest. "Go ahead, tell me I'm a geek. I can take it."

"Are you kidding? Never. I'm tight with those guys too. Beethoven is my homie."

"For real?" Her eyes light up as she laughs.

"Absolutely. I could play Beethoven's Violin Concerto in D on my Stratocaster if you don't believe me. I can hum you a few notes too." I do, and her eyes widen. She drops her hand from her bracelets, and I pat myself on the back for helping her feel at ease.

"I could listen to Beethoven all day long, and I often do."

I laugh. "So it's Beethoven, Broadway, or bust?"

Before she can answer, the bartender slides our drinks over. I thank him and leave a few bills. They don't let me pay here since we play—that's why I make sure to tip well. Also, if I don't, somewhere, someplace, someone online would start a thread that Campbell Mason Evans aka Hart is a shitty tipper.

Mackenzie lifts her vodka tonic. "With the exception of a few awesome nineties tunes, if it wasn't meant to be belted on a stage or played by an orchestra, I probably don't know it."

Before she takes a sip of her drink, I cut in, wrapping a hand around hers, feeling a little spark from that bit of contact. "The nineties rocked and we need to toast." I let go of her hand and grab my bottle.

"To the nineties and no arsenic?" she asks.

I tap my beer bottle to her glass. "I'll drink to that."

She laughs lightly, and it's a pretty sound, one I want to hear from her again. I want to hear other sounds from her too though. Sighs, moans, and groans.

We drink, and then I ask her about her favorite Broadway shows. Soon, our conversation moves on to a discussion on the cultural prominence of *Rent*, the staying power of *Wicked*, and the it-never-grows-old nature of *Les Mis*. She tells me, too, she loved a revival she saw of that show more than twenty years ago, and for a moment, I'm tempted to name-drop. To tell her my brother Miller—a mere ten months younger and nearly my look-alike—and I were in that revival, the one at the St. James. To ask if she liked "Little People," since Miller and I were cast as ten-year-old Gavroche, and she might have seen me singing the one *Les Mis* song I won't ever sing again on account of having sung it every other night for more than a year.

But I'd blow my cover if I said that, so I sidestep it, returning to her. "That must help with your game night—your knowledge of theater—and I can't help but wonder if we'll see you on *Jeopardy!* sometime? With Alex Trebek asking what the most revived musical is or something?"

I start the *Jeopardy!* theme music, and she answers in about two seconds. "What is *Porgy and Bess* with seven times?"

I whistle in appreciation. "Damn, you are more than a pretty face. You're a fount of knowledge."

A faint blush spreads on her cheeks, and it didn't start at the fount of knowledge comment. I'm seeing the nervous side of her again, the side that wasn't sure I was talking to her after our set.

"Thank you," she says softly, fiddling with those bracelets, and the gratitude in her voice makes me wonder if she's not complimented enough. That's an oversight as far as I'm concerned, but it's one I can fix.

"You're gorgeous, and you're welcome," I add.

"You're handsome, and you're talented." She says

it as if she's testing out the words, trying compliments on for size.

I decide to keep it up. "Thank you, and your brain is a turn-on." I wrap a hand around her wrist, settling her busy fingers.

She lets out a breath and meets my eyes. "Thank you, and your ability to play music on request is hot." She adds a coy little smile. She's sexy and clever with a side of awkward. It's such a delicious combination.

"I can play this *thank you and you're welcome* game all night. But . . ." I move closer to her and run my finger along her temple. "But I also want to know something. How do you know all these little facts? Do you have a photographic memory?"

She laughs and shakes her head. "I wish. You really want to know?"

"Is it going to be a freaky weird answer, like you were locked in an attic with only trivia books for a year?"

She taps her nose, then takes a drink.

"Wait. That's it?"

"Not entirely. But close. When I was in grade school, my grandfather told me my brain would shrink if I didn't exercise it every single day. And that didn't mean math or science or reading. It had to be little facts and details."

"Fear is a great motivator."

"Isn't it always? He gave me trivia books for

Christmas, and I gobbled them all up. He'd quiz me on them and dole out rewards for correct answers. A quarter here and there, a cookie for ten in a row. For twenty or thirty, he'd take me out for ice cream. If I earned something like ninety out of one hundred in all sorts of categories, I'd go to a Broadway show."

"Damn, Grandpa didn't mess around. And he wasn't even trying to create one of those quiz-show kids?"

She smacks her palm on the bar. "That's the crazy thing. You'd think he was, but nope. It started as a lark, but I took to it, and that's why he kept it up. He saw it worked for me, so he kept going."

Like me and a guitar. Like me and music. Like my voice and songs. I took to the violin when I was four, the piano at six, microphone when I was eight, the guitar when I was twelve. "My grandmother always said we all have different gifts. The key is to learn how to use yours."

She smiles softly, and it reaches her eyes. "Evidently, my gift is memorizing details in exchange for rewards." She pauses then asks, "What about you? How do you know all the songs? I swear you sang a refrain from everything."

I laugh so I don't have to answer right away. Do I want to tell her the truth? That my brothers and I used to put on shows all the time at home. We started with puppet shows, moved up to made-up plays, then parlayed that into commercials, musicals, and finally, a popular teen duo, then trio, singing in concerts and arenas.

But "I launched my career as a child actor" is not necessarily what you want to say to a woman who has seen you on stage playing guitar.

Guitar equals sexy.

Child actor equals hot mess.

I shrug happily. "I just like music." There's not a shred of a lie in that answer. "And I like that you enjoyed my music," I add, my voice going a little low, a little raspy. I hope she gets my meaning.

She does, her body language speaking for her as she moves closer and flips her hair off her shoulder. I detect a faint hint of nerves in her eyes, maybe a touch of awkwardness, like she's not sure what to do or say next.

But she seems to sort it out when she says, "How long have you been in the band?"

"We started up earlier in the summer. My daughter told me I needed a hobby."

She unleashes a huge grin. "You have a kid?"

I make the scout's honor sign. "I do. No fooling."

"Are you serious?"

Is having a kid a deal-breaker these days? "Does that mean you're about to get a call from a friend saying you need to take off?"

That might have come out more defensively than I expected.

The word *nope* pops out of her mouth. "I have one of those—what do we call them?—kids too."

Ah, now that's interesting. "Single mom?"

She nods. "Single dad?"

I nod, smiling, digging her answer. "As single as the day is long."

"My son is away at camp." The words fall from her lips in a traffic pileup.

But I know how to untangle them. "How fortuitous. My daughter is sleeping at a friend's house."

She nibbles on the corner of her lips. "My friend Roxy thinks I should—"

"—let yourself have a good time for one more night?"

"How did you know?"

"She seemed like a good wingwoman." I reach for a strand of her hair, running my finger across the soft locks, cataloging her reaction. "Want to know what I'm thinking?"

She nods.

I flash her a wicked grin. "I'm wondering if you want to be kissed by someone who's been wanting to kiss you all night long."

A flash of hesitation crosses her face, then she raises her eyes as if she's thinking.

"I do," she whispers, and the few seconds of reticence make her answer even sweeter.

I thread a hand through her hair. I'm going to take my time working up to a kiss, to make sure she wants it desperately. "I've been thinking about running my hands through this hair."

"You have nice fingers..."

"Were you watching my hands when I was on stage?"

Her voice is soft and feathery, a quiet little confession. "Yes. I like the way you play."

"What did you like about it?" I curl my hand tighter around her head. I swear, heat is radiating off her body, and it's so damn enticing. "Did it make you think of anything?"

She nibbles on the corner of her lips. "Made me think about how you might play... me."

A groan works its way up my chest. She is an alluring mix of daring lioness and clumsy puppy. I yank her flush to me, bringing her mouth mere inches away from mine. "I'd like to play your body like a guitar. I'd like to make you sing, make you cry out in pleasure." I run both hands through her soft hair, tugging her head back.

She gasps, and that's my cue to lick a path up her neck, where I nibble on her jaw till she's squirming against me. "Did you think about how I might kiss you when you watched me play?"

A sexy little sigh seems to escape her lips,

followed by a *yes*.

"I noticed you the other week. At your booth, doing your quiz. Couldn't stop looking at you. You were so sexy and adorable, and now you're so damn close to me all I want is to turn you on."

She parts her lips, and there's no more need to tell her what I want to do. It's time to show her.

I slant my mouth to hers and capture her lips. I groan when we connect, and it sparks, that unmistakable match-to-kindling chemistry of an epic first kiss. Lust jolts down my body, and my bones start to hum. Our lips slide together, and we moan in unison. I kiss the corner of her lips then lick inside.

She sighs and presses her body to mine, and we kiss for several deliciously dirty seconds that unspool into a minute, then more. I can't keep my hands off her. Can't stop kissing her. Touching her. Wanting her. Her lips taste like vodka tonic, and her tongue tastes like the woman I want to fuck tonight.

But I'm keenly aware the things I want to do to her should occur in private, behind closed doors. I break the kiss, my breath coming fast and hard. Hers too. "What would you say about getting out of here?"

She wiggles her eyebrows. "I live two blocks away."

That's the sexiest thing anyone's ever said to me.

* * *

When we reach her house, she flicks on the kitchen lights and grabs my shirt collar. "I have to warn you about something."

I steel myself. Warnings before nudity are generally not good. But she smiles like she has a naughty secret. "It's been a long time for me."

Now that's the kind of warning I like. "Is that so?"

She nods and brushes her lips along my neck. She's fiery now that her nerves have packed up and hit the road. "And I think I might be kind of wound up."

"Want me to unwind you?"

"I do, but don't get annoyed if it takes me only a few seconds."

I laugh. "I assure you, there's nothing annoying about that."

She nibbles on my earlobe. "Also, you smell really good."

"So do you."

Her soft mouth reaches my ear. "I kind of want to lick you all over."

Her words send a jolt through me. "That could be arranged."

"Right now?"

I pull back and meet her gaze. Her brown eyes are blazing with desire. "Right now?" I repeat it because I want to be certain of what she's saying.

She runs the tip of her tongue over her bottom

lip then palms my cock through my jeans, rubbing the heel of her hand against my erection.

Yeah, certainty has been achieved. "You don't want me to unwind you first?"

She shakes her head. "Maybe I'm a dirty pervert, but ever since I first saw you on stage, I've thought about three things. Talking to you. Kissing you." She pauses, and I keep my eyes on her, waiting for the final item. She brings her mouth near mine, whispering against my lips, "And how you'll taste when my lips are wrapped around you."

I growl loudly and grip her hips hard. "Fuck, you're dirty."

Her brown eyes widen. "Too dirty?"

"Sunshine, there's no such thing," I say, cupping the back of her head. Her smile reminds me of a perfect summer day. "There's never a thing like 'too dirty' when you're talking about my dick sliding across your tongue."

She trembles. "Good. Because I want that right now."

Gone is the slightest trace of awkward. Out the door are the nerves she showed earlier. She's a woman who knows her mind and her body, and I'm the lucky son of a bitch who gets to enjoy her certainty.

I push her to the floor easily, where she unzips my jeans and tugs down my briefs, freeing my cock.

I'm aching for her to get her hands and her tongue on me.

On her knees, she takes my hard length in her hands, and I hiss when she makes contact.

Lust and desire take hold of me as she strokes. We're on a fast track for a decadent one-night stand, with this dizzying rush of going from flirting to nearly fucking in an hour. Desire thrums under my skin as Mackenzie fists me, bringing the head to her lips and opening wide. She draws me into her mouth. Her lips are pink and full, and they're wrapped around one of my favorite organs.

I groan loudly when she flicks her tongue along the underside as if she's savoring every flavor, like she's tasting a lollipop. This is the most fantastic view I've seen in ages—a gorgeous and smart woman treating my dick like candy.

She moans, humming against my shaft.

I'm toast. I'm roasted, grilled, and flambéed.

But there's one thing that would make this better. One minor detail.

"It's so fucking good, but I want you to suck me deep. Take me all the way."

As she draws me into her hot mouth, I think—no, I'm sure—this is the definition of a real good time.

CHAPTER 5

Mackenzie

Take that, Jamison.

So there, Roxy.

I've still got it.

I mean, it's not like I remember the last time I flaunted it.

But tonight I'm flaunting . . . whatever it is that gets flaunted.

Because Jamison was right.

Sometimes you need to have fun, and this feels like nothing but fun—this dick in my mouth.

But since I have a stranger's yummy cock sliding past my lips, I suppose it's best to let the thoughts of my son's father and my bestie fall from my head like leaves from a tree.

I draw him in deep and lick a delicious stripe up his hard length. I barely know this guy, but I am caught up in the thrill of being on my knees. It's not that I'm submissive. At least, I don't think I am—I honestly don't know what I am when it comes to sex, because my experience in the last decade looks like a map through the Gobi Desert with a watering hole appearing every two to three years.

But I have one active, well-oiled, frequently exercised imagination. It's go time, and I'm putting my mind to practical use.

He grunts and growls, the sexiest sighs of pleasure that spur me to suck harder, play more. Campbell possesses a spectacular dick, and I like the length of him, the taste of him.

Most of all, I like that he's so into me. It's a wild thrill, a welcome respite from the routine of my daily life. And so, I give this blow job my all, since there's no point in giving a half-baked blow job. Besides, I've watched enough Tumblr feeds—okay, countless—and I've picked up a few pointers.

Open wide.
Relax your throat.
Turn your lips into a Hoover.
And don't leave the balls out of play.

It's not rocket science to give a man an earth-shattering blow job. All it takes is commitment, an ironclad effort, and a willingness to go the distance.

I've got that in spades, and I suck him with vigor, eliciting a carnal groan.

"That's so fucking hot."

I'm so fucking hot for him. The ache I feel drives me on as Campbell wraps his big hands tighter around my head, curling them through my hair. His voice is raspy. "Damn, look at you. I want to just keep fucking that hot, wet mouth of yours."

Lust zips down my spine from his filthy words. I've heard about men who are dirty talkers, but I've never come across one in my limited travels. I've never been with someone who's said something so fantastically filthy to me in the heat of the moment.

I reward him with an even stronger suck, my lips ziplocking his cock.

He shudders. "Fuck me. I could come in your throat any second."

His hands drop to my shoulders, and in a heartbeat, he pries me off. Yes, it feels like prying, because I don't want to let go. But I don't want to force my mouth on him. Should probably avoid that. *Forced sucking.* Better look that up and make sure I don't do that.

Pulling me up from the floor, he stares at me with eyes that blaze with desire.

"You're driving me crazy."

Check—I drove a man crazy! You really can learn how to give good head from the internet. "If crazy is good, why did you stop?"

"Because I'd like to take a rain check on the hottest blow job ever, since I don't plan on coming in your mouth for the first time with you."

First time! Does that mean there'll be a second and a third? A girl can dream big.

"Where do you want to come for the first time with me?" I ask it ever-so-innocently.

His eyes narrow into slits. "Do not say that to a man." He kneads one of my breasts through my top. "I want to come everywhere on you. These tits." His hand drops to my ass. "On your ass." His fingers slide between my legs, cupping me through my jeans. "Right now, I think I'd really love to bury myself inside you and feel you on my cock. Think we can make that happen?"

I nod as my world blurs into heat and desire and the need to get naked this second.

We strip, his shirt flying off. My jeans hit the floor, and I push down my panties. I don't even get my top off when his hand slides between my legs. He pushes me back against my kitchen counter and glides his fingers across all my slickness.

"You're not in me," I point out as I moan.

He smirks. "Is it a problem that your sweet pussy distracted me?"

Not in the least.

My mind is white-hot static as he fingers me, peppering kisses on my neck and jaw with each stroke. I grind down on his hand, my hips circling and lowering. It's so rare that you can stop and enjoy a finger bang in the kitchen, rather than a cup of soup.

He hooks his fingers, and my voice rises an octave or ten as I cry out. I was right—it hasn't taken me long to reach O-zone. Here I am. *Nice to see you, climax.*

This orgasm takes no prisoners. It spreads from my center to every cell in my body, demanding each molecule bathes in its deliciousness. I'm moaning and panting as he lifts me up and sets me on the counter. When I open my eyes, he's grabbed his wallet and is tearing open a condom wrapper.

"Now you're even wetter, Sunshine. And I can't wait to feel you grip my dick when I slide into you."

I yank off my top, unhook my bra, and look into his green eyes. "I want you," I say, and I instantly want to smack myself for sounding like a newbie when it comes to dirty talk. I lower my gaze.

He tucks a finger under my chin. "What's wrong, Sunshine?"

"Ugh. That was just so basic—*I want you*—compared to all this delicious smut you weave with your tongue."

Before he removes the condom from the wrapper, he takes my hand and wraps it around his cock. He's hard and pulsing.

"Say it again," he urges.

I knit my brow. "I want you?"

Nothing happens.

He stares at me, his eyes hard and hungry. "Say it like you mean it."

I square my shoulders, look him in the eyes, and whisper, "I want you."

His dick twitches in my palm, thickening more. Holy smokes.

"Feel that?"

I nod.

"Anything wrong with your word smut?"

"I guess not." I smile like a wicked vixen.

"Now, tell me you want me to fuck you hard."

I raise my chin, and say in a husky voice, "I want you to fuck me so hard."

He throbs in my hand, growling curse words as he grabs the latex, throws the foil to the floor, uncurls my fingers, and rolls the protection down his shaft. He tugs me to the edge of the counter. Positioning me so I line up with him, he nudges the head of his cock against me. My knees widen, inviting him in.

He pushes in.

I see *stars*.

With each inch, I die and go to heaven, over and

over, until he's buried to the hilt, and it's like a heavenly host of dirty angels are singing a filthy "Hallelujah."

He brings his mouth down on my neck and bites. I shiver and shudder as he drives deep into me. "Did you want to fuck me the first night you watched me on stage?"

Oh God, he's doing it again. He's melting me in seconds with his words. I wrap my arms around his neck and rock into him, moving as much as I can on the counter. "I came to you later that night."

"That's so hot—you on your bed getting off to me." He moans loudly as he slams into me.

My brain pops and fireworks light up behind my eyes. Pleasure takes control of my body, my thoughts.

His dick far in me.
My wetness on him.
Lips, teeth, skin.
Grind, press, rasp.

"I wanted to do this to you from the moment I saw you. Wanted to fuck you so hard." His words come out staccato as he fucks. He screws like he owns me. Like he knows every inch of my body.

Like I'm ...

It hits me.

He fucks me like I'm his guitar.

He can make whatever music he wants with me.

He can strum any song with his cock and his fingers and his filthy mouth.

I pant as his words turn simpler.

So fucking good.

So hot.

Want you to come.

And I do.

It's like a flash of lightning across the summer sky, and then thunder, and I have no idea right now which one comes first, thunder or lightning, or lightning or thunder, or me.

I cry out as bliss curls inside my body.

When I open my eyes, he has a wild, wicked grin lighting his face. "Hop off and bend over the counter, Sunshine."

That sounds like a command I want to obey. I do as he asked, and he slides back into me and goes to town, gripping my hips, his fingers digging into the flesh of my ass, his cock driving deep.

He owns this fuck. He gives this fuck. He gives all the fucks in the universe. He gives them to me. A spark spreads up my spine, over my shoulders, into my hair.

Then, I feel a sharp smack on my ass. It sends a dart of pleasure through my body. "Oh God."

I'm rewarded with his palm on my ass again.

One cheek. Then the other. A thrust, a swat, a drive, a smack.

He rides me hard, spanking and swatting until I'm coming again.

He grabs my hair in a fist and tugs it, and that caveman act prolongs my orgasm and seems to unlock his. He's rocketing into the same zone, and he's not quiet.

Fuck.

So good.

Fuck me...

Coming so hard.

I believe there's a gold standard now for one-night stands.

Not for me.

But for the world.

No one has ever had a one-night stand better than this.

CHAPTER 6

Mackenzie

We're in my bedroom. I'm not entirely sure how we wound up here. Possibly, this sexy man might have carried me.

As I lie next to him, moonlight filtering through the windows, I posit a question. "Do you know if it's possible to turn into a limp noodle after great sex?"

He strokes his chin. "I believe it takes several orgasms for that to occur."

"Too bad I only had three."

"Three's enough for limp noodle. Four will reduce you to jelly."

"I'm willing to become jelly."

He laughs and nuzzles me, planting a kiss on my throat.

Oh dear. He's cuddly. That's not good because it makes me want to keep him, and I don't think that can happen.

After all, this is one night only, and I'm fine with one night.

He runs a hand along my hip in a way that makes me want one night more. "Incidentally, giving you orgasms is one of the most rewarding things I've ever done."

I arch a brow. "It is? Why's that?"

"You come fantastically."

I cover my face with my hand, a surge of embarrassment rushing through me. "That sounds—"

"Hot? Sexy? Incredible? The way you come is a thing of beauty. You're the most beautiful comer."

I laugh. "That's not a thing."

"It should be."

I prop myself on my elbow, my head in my hand. "Did you know the average female orgasm lasts twenty seconds and the average male one is only six seconds?"

"And yours are sixty seconds?"

I laugh again. "Why do I think you're exaggerating for the sake of your own ego?"

He scoffs. "Sunshine, my ego is solid thanks to

that hat trick. But don't blame me for enjoying giving you triple doses of pleasure."

I smile. "I don't blame you."

He turns to his side, meeting my gaze. I half expect him to grab his briefs, check his Twitter feed, and tell me he has to bounce. Instead, he says, "Tell me another sex fact."

That I can do. Easily. "We just burned two hundred calories. That's the average burn rate for thirty minutes of vigorous sex."

He pumps a fist. "Excellent. Fitness and fucking. A twofer."

"Also, it only requires two tablespoons of blood to get the average penis erect."

"So mine required ten?"

I swat him. "If yours took ten, you wouldn't be inside my body. You'd have ripped me in half."

He drags his fingers from my breasts to my belly. "Glad you're intact."

I set a hand on his chest, feeling his heart beating fast still. "Also, during orgasm, the heart beats at one hundred forty beats per minute."

"And resting is around one hundred, right?"

I nod.

He covers my hand with his own on his sternum. "Is it still beating fast?"

He asks it with surprising tenderness, and a

sweetness that makes my heart flutter. "Yes," I whisper.

For a fleeting second, I wonder if this can be more than a one-night stand. I picture dates and fun times together. Heartbeats and orgasms. Lunches and dinners and trivia nights.

I slam on the brakes.

I can't travel down this road. It's twisty and dangerous. My life isn't arranged for romance. It's not designed for dates. It's perfectly calibrated for being a mom and a business owner, and that's it.

Which is why this path feels even riskier when he places his palm between my breasts and says, "Yours is beating fast too."

It's best to move away from beating hearts. "That was the first crazy thing I've done this summer, and summer's nearly over."

He arches an eyebrow. "This was crazy?"

"Completely crazy. This was my son's first summer away at camp, and I spent most of the two weeks he was gone catching up on movies and working."

"What sort of work do you do?"

"I'm a graphic designer."

He traces my hummingbird tattoo. "Did you design this yourself?"

I nod. "I sure did."

He presses a kiss to it. "It's hot and sexy and drew

me to you like a beacon. Also, I'm glad I could corrupt you with craziness for the night. Being a parent does limit the crazy, right? It's not like you can run out for pizza and beer at two in the morning when you have a sleeping kid."

"Exactly. Usually you want to be asleep too. But there was this one time in June when my son and I went out for milkshakes and fries at the way late hour of ten o'clock at our favorite diner. That felt like the height of insanity."

He smiles. "So wild. If you ever want to go really crazy, you need to try Willy G's Diner in Murray Hill. It has delicious milkshakes and the gooiest grilled cheese sandwich you've ever had."

I put a hand on my belly. "I think my stomach rumbled just thinking about a great grilled cheese sandwich."

"Now I'm thinking about calling Willy G's and seeing if he delivers here."

I laugh. "What about you? Is that the sort of thing you normally do? Grab yummy diner fare late at night?"

He laughs and runs a hand through his thick hair. His voice is a little gravelly, and I like that post-sex sound. "My late-night activities usually involve playing with the band once or twice a week and testing baked goods for my daughter's videos."

"Does she have a baking show?"

"She makes videos for Snapgram. Or Instachat. Or Latergram, or something like that. And I'm her tester."

"That's definitely wild."

"I'm not sure if she does it because she likes baking or likes making videos about baking."

"That's so meta."

"It is, but she's a good kid. I can't complain."

"Mine is as well. He only reads bios of sports stars if they're good guys and treat their wives well and don't have criminal convictions."

"True role models, then?"

"Exactly." I glance down at Campbell's naked frame, the tribal bands on his arms, the sunbursts on his biceps. He's so far removed from my every day, and yet here we are having the most normal of conversations. "I can't believe we're in bed discussing our kids."

He props himself on his elbow. "It's kind of nice."

"Honestly, it is."

"But you know what would be even nicer? If I could put you on your hands and knees and give you a fourth orgasm."

A shudder runs through me. "I'm all for Os, but I thought I was giving you a blow job. That rain check and all?"

He arches a brow. "The way I see it is like this—if

I don't cash it in tonight, that means I can get another date with you."

My body goes still. I blink, then stare at the gorgeous man sprawled out on my comforter. His skin is golden, his arms are covered in ink, and his jaw is neatly lined with stubble. He's a master at playing my body, but I never expected this brand of fun would last beyond one night.

"You want a date with me?" The words come out jerkily.

He laughs lightly. "Is that such a crazy idea?"

"It might be crazier than anything else. I thought for sure this was a one-night stand."

He wrenches away. "Do you want it to be one?"

I don't have to contemplate. I know the answer, even though it scares the hell out of me. I've had the best time tonight, and I want another scoop of ice cream.

It's risky, but maybe I can pull off the balancing act. Two dates won't mess up my neat and orderly life. "I want it to be two," I whisper, my heart racing a little faster.

He smiles and presses a kiss to my shoulder. "Good. I do too." His lips travel across my collarbone, and I tremble as he leaves goosebumps in his wake. "Now, about that fourth one..."

He flips me to my hands and knees, but before he locates a condom, he presses a kiss between my legs.

Ohhhh.

That's something I want to feel again. And again. And again.

I moan like a cat. It's that good, that spectacular. He licks me in this vulnerable pose, one I don't normally imagine myself in. He puts a hand on my back and pushes me down while pressing a hot, wet kiss between my legs that sends electricity all through my body.

When I cry out, he pulls away, hunts for a condom, and spreads me open.

"I think you're ready."

He takes me again.

Oh yes, Mama is having fun tonight. This is an epic end to my summer, and I couldn't be more ecstatic as he rides me to the edge of another orgasm. A few minutes later we lie there, naked and sweaty and sated.

"I've achieved jelly status."

He pumps a fist. "Excellent."

"What comes after jelly?"

"Six orgasms equals brain-turning-to-melted-chocolate-for-a-full-day."

I nod, as if I like the idea. "I'd be amenable."

Then I yawn.

A massive, drive-a-truck-through-it yawn.

"Want me to go?"

"I have to wake up really early," I say.

He slides out of bed. "Let's make sure you get your beauty sleep. But I am very serious about wanting a second date."

Another yawn hits me hard while I'm smiling stupidly. "I want to see you too."

He pulls on his clothes, and I tug on a T-shirt and sleepily walk him to the door. He drops a sweet, soft kiss to my lips, and the tenderness of it tells me this is something more. This isn't a one-night stand at all.

We exchange numbers, and as I open the door, I blurt out, "I never asked more about you being a musician. I was too caught up in your dirty poetry to ask more questions."

The corner of his lips curves up. "I'll tell you more when I take you out. Go to sleep, Sunshine."

One minute later, there's a text from him.

Campbell: Sleep well, and may you have many dirty dreams about me.

I float to my bedroom and engage in the dirtiest of dreams all night long.

CHAPTER 7

Campbell

Ever have sex so good it robs you of the power of rational thought? Yeah, that was me last night.

Maybe I should've told her my other name. Possibly I should've been a little more detailed about what I do. But she didn't really seem to care one way or the other, which was nice. Besides, I can tell her on our second date.

But JJ thinks I should have told her everything, and he's letting me have it as we run the next morning in Central Park.

"I'm just saying she might want to know who you really are."

"I'll tell her when I see her again."

My drummer disagrees with my logic, scoffing. "You know how women are. You truly think she's going to be just fine and dandy learning you're not really Campbell?"

"I am really Campbell. News flash—Mason Hart was a stage name."

"But you're still Mason Hart. It's not just a name."

"I'm Campbell. And Mason is just a name."

He shakes his head as we power up a hill. "Not to women. That shit matters. My wife pretty much demanded to know what JJ stood for on our first date."

"Ouch." My breath comes hard as we near the top of the hill. "Did you tell her?"

He nods. "Hell, yeah. I knew I wanted to see her again. So I laid it all out. 'Just Joking,' I told her."

"Bet that went over well."

He smacks my arm. "Dickhead, I told her it stood for Jonathan Joseph, and I never ever wanted to be called that. She never has, but she appreciated I was upfront. So I bet your girl is going to be a wee bit ticked."

I wave my hand dismissively. "I'll sort it out when I see her again."

"Hope she's not pissed."

"She won't be. This woman was cool."

I picture Mackenzie and her wicked fast brain, her naughty lips, and her eagerness. She was wild and sexy and so much fun. I went into the night expecting nothing but a good time, and I left wanting seconds and thirds.

Sex does fuck with the head.

I should know.

My sneakers slap against the dirt path around the park. "It's not like I lied about anything. Campbell is my first name, and Evans is my last name."

JJ cracks up, clutching his belly as we run. "Yeah, and you went by Campbell while you were serenading millions of teenyboppers and their moms in stadiums and arenas."

I laugh. "I'm not that famous."

"You were back in the day."

I point at him. "Operative words. *Back in the day.* That was then. This is now. That's not my life. That's not who I am. It's not even who I want to be."

"I hear ya. I get that you have some logic operating in your favor. But I still think you should have told her she was about to bang a former teen idol."

"Rather than an aspiring moonlighting guitarist and a violin teacher?"

I'm greeted by another series of guffaws. "Nothing you do is aspiring, Campbell. You were born a music prodigy, and you're still one."

We've been friends since middle school, since I was a runty kid and he was a pimply one, through my years singing and touring with both my brothers, and after the trio broke up.

Since we stopped, I hardly feel like the guy I was before.

In many ways now, I am only Campbell Evans, music teacher and music tutor, teaching violin to some of the most talented students in Manhattan. I'm not the guy who wowed millions when he was seventeen and then tragically lost his daughter's mother when he was only twenty-three.

Now, I'm simply a regular single dad in Manhattan.

Well, for the most part.

CHAPTER 8

Campbell: Good morning, Sunshine.

Mackenzie: Good morning to you too.

Campbell: Did you sleep well?

Mackenzie: Let me put it this way, I'm incredibly sore.

Campbell: I should feel guilty about that, but I can't find it in me.

Mackenzie: I thought you might like knowing that. Caveman :)

Campbell: The caveman in me is grunting triumphantly.

Mackenzie: Also, last night was kind of incredible.

Campbell: Kind of? Only kind of?

Mackenzie: You know it was worthy of eight gold medals in one Summer Games.

Campbell: Dude, did you just give me an easy trivia question?

Mackenzie: You're worried I went easy on you, rather than compared you to Michael Phelps?

Campbell: Fair enough. But I'd like to keep earning those golds in making you scream my name. When can I take you out? Are you free this weekend? Are you busy with your son?

Mackenzie: Can I get back to you on that? I think I can on Saturday night, but let me check. Because I'd like to find time to achieve melted chocolate status with you.

Campbell: I see I've unleashed a monster. :)

Mackenzie: Evidently.

Campbell: Say something dirty to me now.

Mackenzie: Take off your pants.

Campbell: Boom. Instant arousal. You're a rock star.

Mackenzie: Ha, you're going easy on me.

Campbell: Sunshine, it's only easy because we have chemistry. Also, I liked talking to you as well.

Mackenzie: Yeah, it seems your mouth is multi-talented. Looking forward to seeing you again, in clothes and out of clothes.

Campbell: I like the sound of that. It's music to my ears.

CHAPTER 9

Mackenzie

"So?"

The one-word question hangs in the air as I drive on the freeway outside New York City.

"So, what?"

Jamison grabs his coffee cup and dramatically downs some. "Are you going to tell me about your night last night? Did you follow my advice? Did you have fun? Because one look at you, and I see a woman who had fun last night."

His voice is full of knowingness, like he can tell what I did from studying my eyes or something.

"What, exactly, does a woman who had fun last night look like?" I grip the wheel tighter, grateful I can focus on the road and not on him. Jamison has always had the uncanny ability to read me. We met in the common room of our dorm our freshman year of college, reaching for the same bag of chipotle chips on the kitchen counter. We had that instant friendship spark. We could talk about anything over chips, and we did.

He taps his chin, and I feel his eyes on my face, as if he can find the answer to what I did last night while I drive. "Hmm. I would definitely say you have a sort of glow about you I've noticed women usually have after great sex."

I shoot him a searing glance then return my focus to the stretch of highway. "And you recognize this because it's the complete opposite of what I had after you?"

He swats my thigh. "Ooh, mean girl."

"Two-pump chuck."

"Oh please. It wasn't two pumps. It was like four."

I crack up. "See? You did like it! You like girls, you like girls."

He covers his ears and belts out, "La, la, la, I can't hear you."

I slug his shoulder. "Note to Jamison: when you come quickly, it means you liked it. Even if it was with a girl."

He shoots me a withering glare, then lets his

shoulders slump. "All my gay street cred is gone, gone, gone." He pretends to cry.

"There, there. I'd say it'd be our little secret, but your thirteen-year-old son is evidence."

He huffs. "Anyway, who did you like it with last night? Anytime you have a little tryst, you get this happy, dopey look about you."

"I've had that look maybe twice in the last ten years, then?"

He sighs sympathetically. "I'm sorry, Mack. I've been busy. I'm out of town all the time. I know you haven't had the chance to date a lot."

"It's okay," I say softly. "I regret nothing. I'd do anything for him."

He pats my leg. "And you do. You're the best mom. There's no one I'd rather share a kid with. That's why I wanted you to have the chance to get out, and look, you did. Yay you. Now tell me everything."

I laugh. "No way."

I don't want to share the details with Jamison. They feel personal. Campbell was a one-night stand at the beginning of last night, and now he's somebody I'm going to potentially date.

A nervous shudder moves through me, but I remind myself I can handle one date.

One date won't spill over into my mom world. I can schedule it when Kyle is with Jamison, so there's no reason I need to worry. I'll tell Roxy the broad strokes later, but the details are for me and only me at the moment.

The exit looms closer, and I turn on the blinker. "I had a good time, and that was that. Let's talk about something else. When do you take off for your next tour?"

"Ten more days," he says, and tells me details of the show he's putting together as we return to who we usually are—co-parents and friends.

When a song comes on his playlist we both like, we sing along to "Lullaby of Broadway," belting out the showstopper.

"Hey, has there ever been a greater show than *42nd Street*?" I ask when it ends.

"Don't even go there. Don't even say that." He rattles off his favorites. "*Hamilton. Rent. Wicked. Assassins. Sweeney Todd.*"

I shake my head. "*42nd Street* is the greatest of all time. You can't deny it."

"I can't talk to you when you get like this. You get crazy. You get awfully crazy and say these things, and they make no sense."

Before I know it, we're pulling up to the camp, and a new kind of excitement races through me as I cut the engine. I can't wait to see my kid.

We head to the campground and cabins where the kids and counselors are gathered. When I see

Kyle, his dirty-blond hair a thick mess on his head, his brown eyes wide with excitement, I can't hold back a smile. He runs over to me and engulfs me in a hug. A warm, gooey happiness floods me. I love my boy. I love him fiercely, and I'm so damn glad he still lets me hug him. Because nothing will ever be better than his arms around me and him saying, "It's so good to see you, Mom. I missed you."

This is better than sex, better than ice cream, and better than winning trivia. This is the big love I want to cherish always. He does the same with Jamison, and he tells us all the details about how he enjoyed playing with other kids who are passionate about Brahms and Bach too.

A tall man strides over to us, finding us in the sea of parents. He sports a goatee, and a name tag indicating he's a visiting teacher at the camp. "I'm Chris Barinholtz, and I work with the Hudson Valley Orchestra."

"Big Ike's cousin?" I ask, since they share a last name.

"The one and only," he says, proudly. "I'm glad she recommended Pine Notes for your son."

"We are too. It's a pleasure to meet you," I say, and we make quick introductions all around.

"I was brought in for a few special classes, and after hearing Kyle play, I told the camp director that I simply must meet Kyle's parents," he says in a deep, rich baritone.

That kindles my interest. "Oh, well, that's nice to hear."

"And we are so glad to meet one of his teachers," Jamison chimes in.

Chris motions us to step aside, out of earshot of the others. He claps Kyle's shoulder. "Listen. They have a lot of talented kids here at this camp, and I've been coming here as a guest teacher for a few years. Let me tell you something, talent this good needs to be nurtured. When you return to Manhattan, you need to make sure he has the finest teacher."

Jamison nods. "Absolutely. He's been practicing with a violin teacher who played in a college orchestra."

Chris scoffs and holds up a hand. "No. I mean somebody who can really take talent to the next level. Someone who will help him flourish. I have a few people in mind. Would you let me make some calls on his behalf and see if I can help secure someone special for him?"

I beam but let Jamison answer.

"That would be fantastic," he says, since he's always taken the lead on Kyle's musical training. Picking the teachers, that is. Because of his job, he has a nose for the best in the business and is often able to pull strings with his Broadway connections. My job is simpler—making sure Kyle knows when his lessons are. It works for us. "Let me know who you might be able to connect us with. I'd love to hear who you're thinking of."

"I'll email you," Chris says to Jamison.

In the car on the way back to Manhattan, Kyle is a nonstop chatterbox in the backseat. "I met this one kid who also really likes basketball, so that was super fun. We talked about LeBron and our favorite symphonies. It was so cool."

I glance over at Jamison and smile. "It is great to meet someone who shares your loves."

"It sure is," Jamison says, smiling back at me.

We have that in our own quirky, bizarre way.

* * *

We go our separate ways after lunch, with Kyle heading home with me, since Jamison is due back at the office. We spend the afternoon unpacking and sending out clothes to the laundry, playing a tense game of Wits and Wagers before I dive into work while he makes a list of school supplies we need to buy. By early evening, Jamison texts me.

Jamison: First, I have tickets to the Yankees Saturday night. Would love to take the kiddo.

Mackenzie: Sounds fabulous.

Jamison: Second, OMG! Cross your fingers extra hard, missy! The Hudson Valley guy might be able to score us someone fabulous! He just emailed to tell me who he's reaching out to!

Mackenzie: Who is it?

Jamison: I don't want to jinx it. But I have a good feeling it'll come together quickly, and then I will tell you!

I laugh at the note, rolling my eyes. Jamison loves surprises. I write back, telling him I can't wait. But really, what's the big deal? It's not like he's hired the director of the New York Philharmonic. Whoever Chris finds will be fine.

I text Campbell that I can get together Saturday night. He replies quickly.

Campbell: I can still taste you.

Campbell: Also, can't wait for Saturday night.

I shiver as I reread his first note. Then I smile over the second. And as I work on a new design, my mind drifts to what he's going to do to me on Saturday night.

I am such a dirty mama.

CHAPTER 10

Campbell

When I meet up with Miller in the late afternoon, he's testing out his model boat in Central Park. "I am going to crush it in the boat racing leagues this year!"

"Do they have boat racing leagues?" I ask as he radio-controls his blue boat across a lake in the park.

"Yes. And the winner gets a kick-ass gold medal in an all-ages competition in late fall. I've enlisted Jackson as my teammate and he is pumped," Miller says, mentioning the seventeen-year-old he mentors in the Big Brother program.

"I hope you and Jackson beat all those pesky fifth graders."

"They are fierce, and we will have to fight hard. He's

meeting me here in a few. Also, do you know they have kickball leagues now in the park? I signed up for one."

"Will you be able to fit it in with your Monopoly and Battleship competitions?"

"Don't knock it. I happen to like to stay young."

"You're racing a boat with ten-year-olds. You can't get much younger."

He flashes a toothy grin. He has gleaming white teeth, dimples, and skin models would kill for. He knows it too. "And look at my face! I still look twenty-five. Unlike you. You've put on some years."

And all in one night too. "Gee, I wonder how that happened twelve years ago when Julie died."

He smiles sympathetically. "Sorry. Just messing with you. I know you've seen your share of shit. But you're still the second-most-handsome brother of the Heartbreakers."

I tilt my head. "Aww, thank you. I appreciate that. Truly, I do."

"Wait. I meant third. Miles is second."

"Second?" I arch a brow. "Surely he's first."

Miller steers his boat in front of another one and cheers as he beats it in a pretend race only he's running. He sighs, then turns back to me. "Campbell, what would it take to get back together?"

I clap him on the back. He's relentless in his pursuit. "You know that won't happen."

"But you play with the other guys. The Angry Waves."

I laugh and shake my head. "You know the name."

He huffs. "The Gnarly Waters."

"Something like that."

"What do they have that I don't? I am a wizard on the keys, and no one in the whole wide world can harmonize like you and me."

I sigh, a little wistfully, as his idea tugs on a small piece of my music-loving heart. Playing with my brothers was one of the great joys in my life, but there's no room for that now. "You know I love singing with you, but it's all the other stuff that comes with it that I don't want—the expectations. That's what the other guys have. They aren't you and me, bro," I say, wishing I could give him the answer he wants. "But what about Miles? Why don't you and he start it up again?"

Miller rolls his eyes. "He's busy down under."

Miles launched a successful solo career post-Heartbreakers, and he's in the midst of a year-long world tour.

"Eventually the tour will be over. Hit him up."

Miller sighs dramatically. "You know the score." He pats my cheek, then his cheek. "These faces, bro. The world sees us as the Heartbreakers."

"I bet the world would find a way to be good with you and Miles."

He pouts and affixes the saddest face in the world. He rubs one eye and acts as if he's tearing up. "What if I told you I was withering away into a pathetic mess?"

I gesture to him. "I would believe you."

He nods sadly, adding an exaggerated frown, like a kid. "Don't you feel bad for me?"

I chuckle. "You're not terribly good at eliciting sympathy when you're standing here and goofing off. Like you usually are."

"Oh, excuse me. I'm allowed to goof off. That's why I worked my ass off when we were younger."

I roll my eyes. "We both worked our asses off."

"And we both loved it." Miller wiggles his eyebrows as he shoves on the controls of his boat. "I'm just saying those were my happiest days, and you're basically depriving me of ever being happy again."

"Your happiness rests on my shoulders?"

"We could do a reunion tour. Pick twelve cities. We did that when we graduated college. We can do it again."

Miller has played with other bands since we split up a few years after college. He's had some good solo runs. He loves performing, but he's never settled down with one band. He wants it all again—the whole nine yards.

But me? I don't want that lifestyle. I can't risk it.

That's why the Righteous Surfboards is a side gig. I don't want the crazy touring lifestyle of the Heartbreakers. My focus is singular, and it's always been singular since Samantha's mom died when she was only two. No touring. No staying out too late. No life dictated by managers and agents and all the things out of my control.

I want my life to be mine, and I like paying it forward by teaching.

I squeeze my brother's shoulder. "I love you, Miller. But I'm happy doing what I'm doing. I have a packed schedule, and I work with great kids. But you should find a new band. Maybe a new partner to sing with. Why don't you do that?"

He huffs as he steers his boat to the shore. "It's not the same without you."

"But what if it could be better? You know I'll be cheering you on. That's what I can do. I'll be your biggest fan."

But that's not enough for him. He wants so much more than I can give.

I glance at my watch. The person I need to give my all to today is Sam, and she's nearly done with her day as a counselor-in-training at a local arts camp. I tell Miller I need to hit the road.

"Hit the road," he says, crooning one of our tunes. "You want to hit the road with me. Let's go on a road trip, girl, just you and me and the headlights . . ."

I laugh him off.

"I've still got it though," he calls out.

"You've still got it."

As I leave, I pass Jackson, stopping to say hello. "You be sure to keep him in line in the boat races," I tell the kid.

"Don't you worry about that. I'll keep my eye on him," he says with a wink, then I head out of the park.

As I walk away, I hum a few bars, still loving the way they sound.

Those tunes have never fallen out of my head, or my heart. They probably never will.

* * *

The next night, I catch up with Miles on Skype. He calls me from the beach.

"I can't believe you fit in time for your big bro," I say when I see his smiling face on my phone. I lean back into the couch, making myself comfortable as Samantha works in the kitchen on a project she's deemed *top secret.*

"I always have time for you," he says, but a pack

of young women wander past him on the sand, distracting him with their itsy-bitsy bathing suits.

"Earth to Miles..."

He snaps his gaze back to me. "Sorry, man. It's naptime for Ben, so I was enjoying myself for ten seconds."

"Would it be helpful if I wore a bikini?"

"Please never do that," Miles says, then fills me in on his tour and the latest antics of Ben, his five-year-old. Sam jumps in front of the screen and says hi to him.

When he takes off, an old buddy of mine calls and starts raving about a kid he taught this summer.

"We're talking prodigy, Campbell."

"Is that so?"

"Blew my mind. He has a gift, both for classical and modern. Any chance you can fit him in for a test lesson?"

Hmm. My Friday afternoon student did just relocate to Miami...

"I'll give it a shot, but I need to confirm in the morning after I look at my schedule."

"Sounds good," he tells me. "How are things at The Grouchy Owl?"

"Love it there," I say, since Chris connected me with his cousin, who runs the bar. "Favorite place to play so far."

Though that might have something to do with a

certain trivia-loving member of the clientele. I end the call and head into the kitchen, my nose up, sniffing the goodness.

Samantha shoos me out, pointing to the living room. "You are not welcome here. Top secret, I tell you."

I hold up my hands in surrender, and she swats my back with a towel.

"I mean it, Dad. Leave. Get out of here. I need to be in the baking zone."

"I'm going, I'm going. Don't you see I'm leaving?"

"Take your phone, go to the living room, sit down, put your feet up. Do your thing. Listen to your music or your podcasts, whatever it is that entertains you, but I need to focus while I am making our treat."

I do as I'm told.

I kick back on the couch and grab my phone. But I don't listen to a podcast, and I don't crack open a book. I send a text to the woman I'm seeing on Saturday night.

Campbell: What did Beethoven do before composing?

Mackenzie: Is this some kind of throwdown? The answer is dunk his head in cold water.

Campbell: How do I know you didn't turn to Google?

Mackenzie: I'm going to pretend you didn't say that.

Campbell: Because that's like a violation of your basic world order, right?

Mackenzie: Absolutely. I would never do that. It would be like if you lip-synched your songs. Now it's your turn. Tell me some kick-ass songs I don't know that I need to listen to.

Campbell: That's a serious challenge. There are so many great songs. I would say if you're not listening to the Righteous Surfboards, you should be checking out Arcade Fire, Sam Smith, and anything by The Rolling Stones, but hopefully you know that. Rilo Kiley, Jane Black, Johnny Cash. But really, I would think, based on your tastes, you're going to like Top 40 pop music best of all.

Mackenzie: Is that a good thing or a bad thing?

Campbell: Do you mean am I one of those music snobs who thinks listening to something by Katy Perry is a mortal sin? That to be cool you need to listen to only hip indie bands played on alt radio and college playlists, and liking Taylor Swift or Justin Timberlake is akin to ordering a wine cooler instead of Pabst Blue Ribbon on Sunday Funday?

Mackenzie: I would never order Pabst. Ever. Does that automatically make me uncool? I guess I'm cool with that.

Campbell: Uncool is in the eye of the beholder. I thought you were pretty cool with your Beethoven knowledge and your Broadway facts. In fact, I have a fun Broadway trivia fact that I'll share with you on Saturday night.

Mackenzie: Tell me now.

Campbell: It will be worth the wait. But here's your hint—it's about the fifth longest-running Broadway Musical.

Mackenzie: *Les Mis*! Can't wait.

Campbell: Know what I can't wait for?

Mackenzie: Tell me.

Campbell: I cannot wait to get my mouth on you again. And I don't just mean your lips.

Mackenzie: **Fire emoticon**

"Okay, Dad, stop sexting with a woman."

I snap my gaze away from the screen, feeling a splash of heat on my cheeks. "I was not sexting."

Samantha laughs. "I'm right here. I know you're not sexting. I was just teasing you."

Whew. I breathe a sigh of relief.

"Anyway, I'm ready, so log in to Netflix."

I send one quick final text.

Campbell: I have been summoned to watch *American Vandal* by my daughter. Farewell.

Mackenzie: You must obey that summons.

I smile as I set my phone on the table, flicking the laptop open and digging the fact that Mackenzie didn't give me a hard time about hanging out with my kid. Honestly, that's one of the reasons I haven't dated in a while. A woman I went out with more than a year ago, Amelia, didn't like the fact that she was second best to my daughter. Whenever I told her I needed to take off to spend time with Samantha, she'd keep texting. Keep asking questions. Send sexy selfies. Like a shot of her boobs was going to make me ditch taking my kid to her soccer game.

Suffice to say, Amelia didn't last long.

Samantha sits next to me on the couch with a bowl of popcorn and points to it. "This is my new recipe for the most extraordinary kettle corn in the entire universe. But it might also be the worst you've ever tasted."

"I'll be the judge of it."

I dip my hand into the bowl and pop some kernels in my mouth. It's sweet and salty and caramel-crunchy. "It's the best kettle corn in the universe."

We settle in and watch the mockumentary, and even though it's a satire about who drew dicks on cars in a school parking lot, I'm not embarrassed, and she's not either, because it's fucking awesome that she still likes to hang out with her dad.

CHAPTER 11

Mackenzie

The train rumbles into the station across town, and with my hand on Kyle's back, next to his violin case, we exit the subway. As we walk along the platform to the stairs, weaving through Friday afternoon crowds, the recognizable notes of U2 sound from a saxophone. Even someone like me can recognize U2's "Mysterious Ways."

Kyle's smile stretches wide as he points to a twenty-something goateed guy blowing into the instrument. A young woman with long, silky black hair accompanies him on a cello.

"Those two are so cool. They play all these old songs."

"Old?" I ask as we walk toward the duo playing on the edge of the platform.

"You know, the kind people like you listened to back in the day. They're the best," Kyle says, his eyes a little glazed as he listens.

I raise an eyebrow. "Excuse me? Old people?"

He nods. "Yeah. People of your generation. The people who listen to oldies music."

I cringe. As a child of the 90s, it still breaks my heart that that decade's music is now considered "retro," and I will do whatever it takes to eradicate that ageist assumption.

"For the record, young man, that's not old. I was raised in the heyday of Nirvana, Pearl Jam, and U2's *Achtung Baby*, which was released in 1991, when I was but a wee second-grader."

"That makes you old, Mom," he says, telling it like it is, like I haven't already been insulted by all the oldies 90s radio stations and playlists. "But don't let it get to you. I like music that's way older. That's centuries older. Would that make it older than dirt?"

I laugh as we walk. "Touché."

He reaches into his jeans pocket and drops a couple bills into the open cello case of the young woman. She nods and whispers a quiet "thank you" as she continues to play.

"That was nice of you to give her some money," I say as we head upstairs.

"She's a student. She's getting her BFA at Julliard."

"How do you know that?"

"My friends and I see the two of them there when we take the subway after school. She's busking a lot at this station."

I wonder, as I have before, if that's going to be his fate. Street performing isn't a bad choice, I suppose. Buskers can be happy with what they do. But I'm also completely aware that finding success as a professional musician is akin to finding it playing professional sports. Will he be the exception? Can he nab a spot in an orchestra or in the pit for a Broadway show? Maybe play jingles for commercials? I have no idea if he'll be talented enough or driven enough.

And that's why I have to remind myself he's only thirteen. He might have dreams and aspirations, but in the end, he could decide to be an environmental scientist or an artist or something else entirely. My role is simply to nurture his hopes right now. Whether they turn into his career is for the future to decide.

That's why I'm taking him to the first lesson Jamison set up with the new teacher. He emailed me about an hour or so ago to tell me the guy that Chris had been courting had an unexpected cancellation and could fit Kyle into his schedule today.

His name is Mason Hart. The Mason Hart.

That's what Jamison wrote.

The name only rang a minor bell for me—something about a boy band of brothers from years ago. But I can google him after the lesson to refresh my memory, since there's no time to do it beforehand.

We make our way through the Friday afternoon crowds in Chelsea and arrive at Jamison's building a few minutes before one.

I say hello to the doorman.

"Hey, Mac and Cheese and Kyle the Machine," Joey says in his Jersey accent, shooting us a lopsided grin. Joey likes to give nicknames.

"Hi, Joey the Terminator," Kyle replies, getting into the game.

The uniformed man offers a fist for knocking. "You know it. Hit a grand slam in my softball game. Terminated the opponents."

"Excellent," Kyle says approvingly.

As soon as we arrive on the fifth floor, Jamison is waiting at the door, practically bouncing on his feet. "I am so excited. I cannot wait for you to meet the new violin teacher. Come in, come in, come in."

Once we head inside, Kyle takes his violin out of its case then rubs his hands against his jeans, a sign that he's a little bit nervous. I think it's a good thing to be a little nervous before you meet a teacher. Kyle excuses himself for the bathroom.

I give Jamison a nudge. "So, you're getting former pop stars to teach violin?"

"Isn't it wild? I loved his music so much. But don't worry. He's a terrific teacher. He cut his teeth on classical music well before pop, so he's no one-trick pony."

"Is he a two-trick horse?"

"More like a full musical stallion," Jamison says with a wink.

"Well, giddy up, then."

Jamison laughs and whinnies like a horse. "*Neigh.*"

There's a knock on the door.

"All right, let's meet this stud," I say.

Jamison practically trots over and flings open the door, as I drop my purse on the counter.

"I am so delighted to meet you, Mr. Hart. Let me introduce you to Kyle's mom."

"Great to meet you."

My spine tingles.

That voice.

Am I hearing things?

I spin around, the hair on my arms standing on end.

My jaw clangs to the floor, full-on Acme cartoon-style.

I've already met the musical stallion, and he's a thoroughbred, all right.

He's a champion racehorse with many tricks under his saddle.

CHAPTER 12

Mackenzie

Let's try to apply logic to this *Twilight Zone* moment.

How is it possible for the hottest one-night-stand-about-to-become-a-second-date to *also* be my son's new music teacher?

Am I being punked? How does being punked even work? And who would be the punker in this scenario? Fate?

Clearly, this is that bitch's idea of a real good laugh.

Take the best sex of my life, add in a great post-coital conversation, layer in a few tender moments, spice it up with some fun text message exchanges over the last few days, then shake it in a blender with some "sorry, sucker" seasoning that ruins the whole milkshake.

And I really like milkshakes.

My shoulders slump, and all my hope of ever having another chocolate milkshake is dashed by the worst stroke of luck ever. Like, in the entire history of the universe, since letting myself have a second date is a very big deal.

Correction: *was*.

There will be no second date because the universe is screwing with me.

Or else Big Ike and her cousin are having a good old guffaw at my expense. I can't believe the guy her cousin recommended as a teacher is also the guitarist in The Grouchy Owl's band.

Campbell stares at me with a stoicism in his green eyes and a stern set in his features that tells me he must be shocked too. He's doing everything he can to hide it. He doesn't want to let on in front of Jamison, and I could kiss him for that.

But that's not saying much. I could probably kiss him for anything. He's insanely kissable.

"Hi-i-i-i-i," I say, and it comes out dry and comprised of five syllables. As I shake his hand, I try to form words again. "I'm ... Mackenzie. Kyle's mom."

"I'm Campbell Evans. Nice to meet you, Mackenzie," he says, his voice a little gravelly, as if he's trying to figure out how this mix-up happened too, even as we both do our best to sweep our little clandestine history under the rug.

But honestly, I do want to know why he's two people. Why he's here to teach my son, and why his naughty texts are on my phone. We stare at each other for another few seconds, saying with our eyes that what happened in my kitchen stays in my kitchen.

Jamison is not one for awkward introductions though. He jumps in and grabs my arm. "Mack, aren't you excited? Is that why you're all awkward? Oh wait." He clasps his hand over his mouth for a second then points at me. "You totally had a teen crush on him too."

Bug-eyed, I snap my gaze to Jamison. "What?"

"You had to have had a crush on Mason Hart of the Heartbreakers. That's why you're all flustered, right? You told me as much in college."

I crease my brow. "I did?"

Poster.

My bedroom.

That man.

Oh, my stars. It's all coming back to me. I was a freshman in high school when his teenybopper band was the rising star of radio, and he and his brother were stone-cold foxes.

My eyes widen, and I stare at the man who plays guitar like he fucks and fucks like he plays guitar.

Wait. That's not helpful, brain.

"You're *the* Mason Hart?" I croak out. "Teen singing sensation, part of the young singing duo-turned-trio who played with his brothers and had three platinum albums?"

Campbell shoots me a lopsided grin, and it's a smile that charmed millions two decades ago. I slip back in time and images flicker in front of me—the too-handsome-to-be-real brothers in their music videos, in teen magazines, all over the radio.

"Yes, but I don't go by that name these days, to be honest. You can just call me Campbell, and I'm totally happy to focus on the present." His tone makes it clear—Jamison needs to back off the hero worship.

That's not the only thing we'll have to back off from. We'll have to back off from . . . *everything*.

Before the moment becomes swollen with any more feet in its mouth, Kyle emerges, a shy smile on his face as he strides up to Campbell.

"Hi. I'm Kyle Markson. Nice to meet you." He extends his hand to shake.

Campbell turns away from me, giving all his focus to Kyle. "Campbell Evans. Great to meet you. I hear you're quite a whiz on the strings. Why don't you play me your favorite song so I can see what we're dealing with?"

And that's how the music teacher defuses the tension bomb—by focusing on the student. The two of them head to the living room, and Kyle picks up his instrument and gets to work.

Jamison and I leave the apartment to give them space to do their lesson without us hovering.

"Can you believe he teaches music?" Jamison asks as we hit the street. "He can play the violin like a maestro."

No surprise. He played my body like a goddamn Stradivarius.

"He does know how to teach, right? Please tell me you didn't hire him because you had a crush on him in middle school?"

Jamison rolls his eyes. "Puh-leeze. Give me some credit."

"Well? I barely heard a word about his credentials."

Jamison stares at me as we walk along his block. "Darling, can't a man get excited about something? Yes, obviously Campbell Evans has big, fat credentials. The man has a Bachelor of Fine Arts from Julliard, for crying out loud. I wouldn't have hired him just because he's a rock star, or because he knows Big Ike. But hello! He is a rock star! Those are two pretty impressive qualifications."

I huff. He's right. I really shouldn't be doubting the man's résumé. He possesses some serious music chops. "I just want to make sure he can teach violin," I say, because that's true. The things he did to my body aren't proof that he's competent at anything but bestowing earth-shattering Os.

Admittedly, though, he's a god with the guitar. That I know for a fact.

"Yes. Look up his bio if you want. He started playing violin at age four. He plays nearly a half-dozen instruments, Mack. He's one of those all-around musical superstars. He definitely knows what he's doing."

I slow my pace as I google Mason Hart.

Images pop up first, and my pulse spikes as I stare at a carousel of shots. I'm like a dirty old woman perving on a teenager, but holy smokes. Teenage Campbell was crazy hot. With the thickest head of hair I've ever seen, and just that perfect amount of forehead flop, his locks could not have been more tailor-made for a pop sensation. But his face was to die for. His jaw looks like it's never met a blade, and he's bathing in fresh-faced, boyish charm. He's so dang good-looking and swoony in a *Tiger Beat*, teenage-wet-dream kind of way.

But he's also quite different from adult Mason. Or Campbell, I should say. With sinewy muscles, inked arms, delicious stubble, and sexy-as-fuck crinkles around his eyes, he's handsome as hell now.

And all man.

One hundred percent rough, sexy, dirty man.

And I can't sleep with him again.

A tear pricks the back of my eye. Or maybe that's my sex drive crying me a river and cuing the sad trombone. "How is it that a former pop star becomes a music teacher?" I mutter as I stuff the phone back into my pocket.

"From what Barinholtz told me, he always planned to teach. Pay it forward, if you will." Jamison slows at the corner and stops, leveling me with his gaze. "Do you have a problem with him, Mack?"

Uh-oh.

Time to dial down the inquisition. Time to turn it all the way off. If I let on I know Kyle's new teacher in the biblical sense, Jamison will never let me live it down. I shake my head and fasten on an all-is-well smile. I don't want Jamison to know the new teacher is the reason I was glowing on the ride to camp.

"I was just surprised and processing everything. But he looks great," I say, waving my phone. "His bio is compelling."

So are his photos.

"He really is talented, and he's built a reputation as a stellar teacher," Jamison adds, resuming our pace.

"He seems totally stellar." *In the sack.*

"I think as long as Kyle gets along with him, he'll be a great choice, and that's not simply because of his background. But I did get a kick out of who he was."

I got a kick out of him fucking me, and now that's over.

"I completely loved the Heartbreakers," Jamison continues. "Sometimes I still listen to their tunes."

"Oh yeah, me too," I say lightly, even though that's not true. I can't remember the last time I heard one of their songs.

"Good. Because I was worried there." Jamison grabs his beeping phone from his pocket and swipes his finger across the screen before grimacing. "Crap. I need to get to the office. Our leading lady sprained an ankle, and we open in a week."

I shoo him toward the nearest subway. "Go, go. You must save *Chicago*."

He drops a kiss to my forehead. "Let me know how everyone thinks the lesson went, and if we should keep it up."

"Of course," I say, then I wander around his neighborhood for the rest of the hour, my mind occupied the whole time with disappointment that my date on Saturday can't happen. Dating my son's music teacher would be a Bad Idea. If things didn't work out with us, I'd be stuck seeing him for every lesson. It would be awkward for me, but potentially worse for Kyle. I don't want to risk him losing a shot at working with a musical genius just because I want to bang that teacher. And I don't want to fire Campbell simply so I can sleep with him. That seems a tad, how shall we say, *selfish*?

I return to Jamison's building, using my key to let myself into the apartment.

As soon as the door opens, Kyle's laughter meets my ears. "That's awesome. I've always wanted to learn that song."

"If you can master the Brahms, I will teach it to you."

"Promise?" Kyle asks.

"Dude. Consider it a blood oath."

"All right. I'm holding you to it."

A smile stretches across my face as I watch Campbell shake hands with my son.

"How did it go?" I ask.

Please say it was awful and you can't imagine working together, and that moment I just witnessed was the only time you got along during the entire lesson.

WAIT. *Bad Mackenzie.* Don't wish for that.

Kyle beams. "It was awesome. He listened to me play, and then he showed me how to mesh Bach with Jay-Z."

Campbell shrugs. "Just some rock melodies that sound pretty rad on the violin."

Kyle laughs. "You do know no one says 'rad' anymore, right?"

Campbell scratches his head. "Nope, but I hear I'm not cool either. That's what my daughter tells me."

I suppress another smile as I think of our text exchange last night. Neither one of us is cool at all.

Campbell locks eyes with me, and a thousand dirty thoughts flash through my mind. Him bending me over the counter. Fucking me on the counter. Putting me on my hands and knees on my bed.

Those images slip and slide with others. The tenderness he showed in bed when we talked. The questions he asked me. The texts we shared about music, trivia, kids, and more.

We connected physically, but we also started to spark emotionally. He's the first man I've been this excited to go on a date with in years.

As he talks about Kyle's potential, his raw talent, and where he sees him going, I can tell exactly why Campbell's good at teaching—there's a confidence, an ease, and an excitement in his voice. I can tell, too, that Kyle likes him, since he's listening, and nodding, and smiling.

"That sounds great. I'll talk to Kyle, and I can circle back to confirm another lesson," I say, and the subtle message should be clear—I want to make sure the kid likes him too.

But the kid cuts in. "Mom, it's all good. I like Campbell. I'm ready to schedule more lessons. You don't have to quiz me privately to find out what I really thought. He challenged me in ways no one has in a long time, so I'm cool with him."

I laugh. "Way to blow my cover."

Kyle smiles as he grabs his violin case. "Taylor just texted me. We snagged an extra hour today to practice at the community center, and then we want to play some video games at his house. Can I go see him before dinner?"

"Get out of here," I say, gesturing to the door, glad he wants to both make music and hang out with his friends in his string quartet. The community center is close enough that he can walk. "I'll swing by Taylor's house later to get you."

He scoots out, and that leaves me alone with the man I want to date but can't.

Silence cocoons us. Awkwardness slinks between us. I stand five feet away from the man who's seen me naked, and I'm dying to know what he's thinking and if his thoughts are as discombobulated as mine.

Campbell holds my gaze. "Of all the gin joints in all the towns in all the world."

"Yeah, some luck this is," I say, dejectedly.

"I had no idea you were his mother."

"Yeah, same here." I tap my chest. "Well, I know

I'm his mother, but I had no clue you were going to be his teacher."

His voice is soft and caring when he crosses the living room and sets his hand on my arm. "Would you rather find another teacher? I understand if you don't want me around, if it feels too weird. But I meant what I said. I've never seen a kid with such raw talent."

I groan, wishing he'd say anything but that. I mean, I do want that. I just wish this weren't so frustrating. "How are you a pop star, and a guitar player, and a music teacher?" I blurt out, because I'm still amazed he's a triple threat.

"I was going to tell you all of that on Saturday night."

"You had your talking points mapped out for our date?"

"I was worried that without them we'd have nothing to say," he says drily. "But to answer your question in a nutshell, I'm really musical. It's in my blood. It's in my soul. I can play five instruments. I started with violin at age four, added piano at six, and then decided I wanted to learn guitar because it was cool. Picked that up when I was twelve. Added bass after."

"That's definitely a prodigy."

He shrugs sheepishly.

"What's the fifth instrument though?"

He wiggles his eyebrows. "Wait till you see me play the glockenspiel."

I crack up. "Now I'm even sadder, since that would have been quite a sight—you on that tiny little instrument."

"But like I said, I can step aside if you prefer."

Is he asking if I'd rather date him instead of keeping him as my son's teacher? "Do you mean you'd step aside so we could date?" I ask, but even as I say the words, they sound horribly selfish and completely antithetical to who I am as a mom. I was barely giving myself permission to date him when he *wasn't* my son's new teacher.

"But even if you didn't want to date, I could excuse myself, if you will, if any of this made you uncomfortable," he says, gesturing from him to me.

I drag a hand through my hair. The prospect of dating him is far too delicious for my own good. But if he canceled as the teacher, I'd have to explain to Jamison and Kyle, and really, it's far too new a thing between Campbell and me for that kind of conversation. *Hey, I fired our teacher since I banged him and want to see if there's anything there besides a second or third screw. K, thanks.*

I sigh heavily, and the sound is laced with regret. "Look, as much as I want to see you again, in every sense of the word, I don't want you to step aside. But

I think *we* are going to have to step aside, if you know what I mean."

He sighs, but smiles too, in acknowledgment. "I get that."

"I need to do what's best for Kyle, and being involved with his new teacher isn't a great idea. His school's music program isn't terribly good, so we like to make sure the people he works with outside of school are top-notch."

He holds up his hands. "Hey, the fact that your kid comes first is yet another reason I like you so much." He snaps his fingers. "Oh wait, I can't like you anymore. I'll just forget I've seen you naked and coming hard in my arms."

"Campbell," I chide, but I'm fighting back a grin, "you can't say things like that now."

"I can't?" he asks innocently. "But I just did."

I wag a finger at him. "You're naughty."

He steps closer. "So are you, and that's why I'm not going to easily forget how enticing you look with my dick in your mouth. But I'll do my best."

A shudder wracks my body as I stare unabashedly at his gorgeous lips. "I'll try to pretend I don't know how filthy your mouth is."

And we're right back to flirting, which we shouldn't do.

"Should we talk about the lessons? How this will work?" I try to focus on being responsible.

"We should. But I have one more question first." He inches closer and runs his fingers down my arm, making me shiver. "Where was the poster of me? On the wall or above the bed?"

I release a shaky breath. "Above the bed."

CHAPTER 13

Campbell

I let that image linger for a little bit longer—a teenage Mackenzie daydreaming about me. Yeah, that's wildly inappropriate, but completely awesome. Not gonna lie.

I shake the thought away, though, because I'm more curious about the present-day woman.

I lift my chin. "So . . . Jamison?"

She slashes a hand through the air as she heads into the kitchen, answering quickly. "We're not together."

Laughing, I shake my head. "I'm clear on that. I also figured as much since you have separate places, and on account of you taking me to your home the other night and fucking my brains out."

Her eyes pop out and she points at me. "Hey. You fucked my brains out. Please get the order of brain-fucking right. Also," she says, tilting her head to the side like a curious pup, "why is it called fucking your brains out? Is that the least attractive metaphor for sex ever?"

I hold up one finger. "Technically, the least attractive would be fucking the shit out of someone."

She cringes and makes a gagging sound. "How did that ever become a saying?" She holds up two mugs from her spot at the counter. "Green tea?"

"Yes, please. And I don't know how that became a saying. Maybe I don't want to know. But instead, let's just say I fucked you senseless three times. Is that better?"

She screws up the corner of her lips as she sets a kettle on the stove. "Don't shortchange me. Wasn't it four? I don't want you to retroactively take away my fourth orgasm."

I shoot her a look. "Don't you know, Mackenzie? Orgasms can never be removed retroactively. The Council of Orgasms deems all climaxes everlasting."

"I love the rules of the Council of Orgasms. Anyway, it was damned impressive. You were damned impressive."

"You were."

"No, you were."

"*We* were."

"Fine, we were. Also, to answer your question, Jamison's gay. I don't know if you realized that."

I scratch my jaw as I move to the counter. "I sort of picked up on that. The poster comment and so on. Were you together and then he came out?"

She scoffs. "God, no."

I crease my brow. "You say that like it's the most absurd thing ever. That does happen."

She nods as she fiddles with the kettle. "I'm well aware that it does happen, but in this case, we were best of friends, and if you ever want to know the height of stupidity or the profound depths of friendship, it would be me giving my bisexual bestie a chance to see if he liked girls one drunk night in college, and then getting pregnant because of it."

I can't help it. I chuckle. That's too much. "That would indeed be the definition of friendship, to lay your body down like that. But it's cool you can be such good friends and co-parent."

"I'm lucky. There's actually no one I'd rather have a kid with. Is that weird?"

I shake my head. "No, it's not. It makes complete sense. Families can come about in the most unusual ways."

The kettle whistles, and she turns it off then pours. "I'm sure it's easy to say now because I have my kiddo—and look, we can all go ahead and admit I have the most amazing kid in the world, because I do," she says with a huge smile. "But it all worked out in a weird and wonderful way."

As she heads into the living room with the mugs, I make my way to the couch. "It does seem like it worked out for you. Have you been with anyone else since? Ever marry?"

Shaking her head, she takes a seat next to me and blows on the steaming mug. "I've dated here and there. Over the years there were a couple guys, but none who I truly connected with on a meaningful level."

I nod, understanding completely. "That's how it's been for me, too, since Samantha was little. I've dated, but I haven't really found anybody who totally gets the situation."

She clears her throat. "What about you? I have to confess, I'm not a big celebrity news person. I don't really know the story of you and your kid."

A smile sneaks across my face. "I love that you're not a celebrity news junkie," I say, running my finger down her arm. That's probably something I shouldn't do. This kind of contact is something I should resist, but touching her feels so natural. Her humor, her wit, her kindness, and her ridiculous sexiness make me want to get my hands on her. "In fact, I love that you had no clue who I was."

"It's not that easy to connect the dots. You're . . . what? Thirty-four?"

I gesture to the ceiling with my thumb. Go higher. "Thirty-five."

"My point. You're thirty-five, not seventeen. You don't exactly look the same."

I pout then take a drink of the tea as I let go of her arm.

She taps her chest. "Nor do I! It's okay if we don't look like our teenage selves."

"True. I didn't have all this ink when I was a teenager." I hold out my arm. She stares at the tattoos on it then traces the string of musical notes wrapped above my elbow and the sunburst on my bicep.

"This is beautiful. I love the sunburst. It's so bright and brilliant. That's some fantastic design work."

"It is, but you know what's even better?"

"What?"

I reach my hand over my head, grabbing at the hem of my shirt. In one swift move, I tug it off.

Her eyes widen. "Campbell," she whispers.

"Don't worry. I'll put it back on." I turn so she can see the back of my shoulder. "You probably missed it the other night."

She gasps. "That is the best Sam-I-Am ever." Her fingers dart out, and I can feel her traveling along the illustration of the Dr. Seuss character wearing a red hat and holding a plate of green eggs and ham.

"I had that done when she was three. It was her favorite book. I read it to her probably ten times a day. At least it felt that way."

"'Would you eat them in a box? Would you eat them with a fox?'" she says softly.

"'Not in a box. Not with a fox. Not in a house. Not with a mouse,'" I answer, relaxing into her touch as she outlines my ink.

"'I would not eat them here or there. I would not eat them anywhere,'" we say together.

Her hand drops. "Great ink."

"Thanks." I tug the shirt back on and turn around to face her. "Your hummingbirds are pretty awesome too." And because they're peeking out her collar, I dive in for a quick kiss, pressing my lips to the birds then licking across them.

She trembles as I kiss her. "We're not supposed to do this."

"I know, but they're so damn alluring, and I didn't get to kiss them the other night." I kiss my way up the birds, inhaling her sweet skin, savoring the way she responds to the barest of kisses. It pains me to stop, but I manage to pull away, doing my best to play by the rules.

She brushes her hands against her thighs. "Well, I'm not hot and bothered at all."

I wiggle my eyebrows. "Me neither."

"My point, before you played dirty, is that you didn't have all this sexy, manly stubble in your teen days, or the laugh lines I happen to think are mega hot. I did look you up during the lesson." A sheepish look crosses her face.

"You were checking me out when I was a hot teenager."

She shrugs as if to say *what can you do?* "You were a totally hot seventeen-year-old. I told you I had pictures of you on my wall, so I had to check you out after you showed up here." She grabs her mug and takes a drink.

"Did you compare me to my younger self?"

"Look, my younger self perved on your younger self, and my older self pervs on your older self. I think the man you are now is hot as sin, but we're not supposed to be going there."

I groan and take a sip of the tea. I wish we were going there. But I get it. I do get it.

"Also," she says, gently, "I have the feeling you didn't want me to ask what I asked you. Is it an off-limits topic I shouldn't bring up again?"

"No." I shake my head and finally answer her. "Sam's mom died when she was two."

"Oh, I'm so sorry." She reaches forward and squeezes my hand, a kind gesture. "That must've been so hard."

"It was at the time. We were married for three years, and the band was still together, though not playing as often. But we toured into our early twenties, for Miller and me at least, since we're older than Miles. That was really hard on Julie, my late wife. After Sam was born, it was even harder. Julie wound up suffering from postpartum depression."

Mackenzie's expression is etched with sympathy. "That's so tough. I didn't experience it myself, but I've heard it can be an awful thing."

"'Awful' is exactly the word to describe it." I shudder, recalling those dark days when I had no clue how to help my wife. "I had no idea what to do. She was completely depressed. Honestly, I think the postpartum depression probably never ended. It carried over to regular depression. She was taking meds, and she really struggled when I was out of town. I tried to set it up so she'd have her family or her sister around and she wouldn't be alone, but it wasn't enough."

I take another drink of the tea, grateful for the distraction of the beverage. It's been more than a decade, but some stories are always hard to tell. "One night, she took too many pills, along with some other meds she had. It was lethal. Her sister came over early the next morning to help, and discovered Sam playing alone in her room, waiting for her mom to wake up. Her sister found Julie in her bed."

Mackenzie clasps her hand to her mouth,

holding in a sob as a sheen of wetness crosses her brown eyes. "That's so sad, Campbell. I'm so sorry for your family, and that you and Julie and your daughter went through that. It's so tragic."

"That's exactly what it was. I blamed myself. Really beat myself up over it."

She pulls back and stares at me sharply. "But it's not your fault, Campbell."

"It felt like it was at that time."

Her voice is firm. "No. It's not your fault. People are wired in certain ways. We're not responsible for somebody else's mental health. You did everything you could for her."

I know what she's saying is true, but a small part of me always wonders. "Sometimes I would think I should have stayed home. Not toured at all."

"But that's not how we're supposed to live our lives. You're not supposed to have someone you love under house arrest."

"I know that now. It was hard at first, but I really do know that now."

She reaches for my hand and clasps it. It's not sexual. It's comforting. "That must have been so hard, to be twenty-three and have a baby girl to take care of all on your own."

"Sam got me through it. Taking care of her was my top priority. I had to focus on my life." I picture Sam as a little girl, wanting me to take her to the park, to play with dolls and trucks, to make cookies with her. "Raising Sam helped me stop missing her mom so much and carve out a new life. It was a long time ago, and I learned over time how to move on."

Mackenzie's smile is gentle, full of understanding. "I don't know if it's fair to expect anyone to ever truly be over a loss like that, but I'm glad for your sake you feel that way."

"But that's why the band broke up," I add, tapping my chest. "I ended the band. I didn't want to play anymore like that. Didn't want that lifestyle."

"Is that why you teach?"

I shake my head. "I always wanted to teach. That was the plan when I went to college. Everything moved faster in the teaching direction when I became a single dad. I wanted to be there for Sam. Not miss a thing."

Mackenzie squeezes my hand. "And now look what you've done. You've made this incredible second career as a fantastic teacher. I'm excited Kyle is going to be working with you. He really lit up at the end of the lesson."

"He did. He was a blast to teach. I'm psyched to work with him. He's a good kid."

As we drink our tea, we talk more. I ask her questions about her graphic design business, and she tells me about some of the projects she's worked on over the years for ad agencies, boutiques, authors, web designers, and more.

"Did you always want to work for yourself?"

"No, actually."

That surprises me. "Explain."

"Well," she says, a look of chagrin on her face, "I planned to work at an ad agency, and I had a job lined up after graduation, but then this happened." She makes a basketball-size arc with her hand over her belly.

"You didn't take the job?"

She shakes her head. "The hours would have been too brutal with a newborn, so I lived with my parents the first year after college, saving up money by doing freelance graphic design at night. After a year or two, I had enough clients to move into the city, get my own place, and build out my business, but it took a little while."

"That's impressive."

She narrows her eyebrows. "It's impressive that I had to live with my parents and a newborn?"

I laugh, shaking my head. "It's impressive you pulled all this off, Mackenzie. You weren't planning for a kid, but you made it work, and you paved a whole new path to your career."

"Maybe." She shrugs.

"Hey, it's not a maybe. It's a hell yes. And it's awesome."

A small smile sneaks onto her face. "Thanks."

"Were you one of those kids who was always good at design?"

"I was a champion doodler," she answers, holding her chin up high. "I doodled constantly in school. I could have taught a master class in doodling."

"Is that so?"

"I doodled on absolutely everything. All over desks and notebooks. They called me Mackadoodle."

"Mackadoodle," I say, letting that sound roll around on my tongue. "That is the best nickname I have ever heard. You are Mackadoodle from now on. You can't be anything else."

She rolls her eyes. "I will not answer to Mackadoodle."

I lean closer and bump my shoulder to hers. "I will get you to answer to Mackadoodle. If I have to wear you down with—"

I can't wear her down with kisses like I want.

"Kisses?" she whispers softly.

"Kisses we can't have."

"No more kisses," she says with a frown. "From now on, you are only my son's violin teacher."

I roam my eyes over her, enjoying the view of her tight, trim figure, her lush hair I've wrapped my hands in, her freckles that somehow are the height of adorably sexy. "And you are my student's ridiculously hot mom that I fucked and still want to fuck."

She shivers. "When you say things like that, you make it that much harder."

I glance at my crotch. "Oh, it definitely is much harder. It got much harder in the last ten seconds when I thought about fucking you again."

She swats my thigh. "You're really naughty."

"You're really tempting, Mackadoodle."

"You're tempting too, Mason Hart," she says, and I drop my jaw in mock surprise over the name. "But we have to be good. We agreed to be good."

I nod. "We will be good. We will be so good at not fucking each other."

She raises a fist in victory. "We will be the best at not fucking each other."

I let myself savor one last look at the gorgeous woman by my side. "On that note, I really ought to leave because if I stay another second, I'm going to try to fuck you on your not-exactly-an-ex's couch." I stand. "And if that happened, I'd have to fire myself on his behalf."

She raises an eyebrow in a question. "Why on his behalf?"

"A man's couch is sacred."

CHAPTER 14

Mackenzie

I am serenaded by Bach and Jay-Z all day Saturday as I work on a new design for an ad agency client. Kyle stops playing for lunch—my world-famous turkey with avocado toast is the star of the meal—and a quick jaunt to the office supply store around the corner for a few last-minute school items. Then we're back at the apartment, and he insists on showing me the mash-up he's been working on since yesterday.

I park myself on the couch and give him my undivided attention for a few minutes of aural goodness.

I cheer and clap at the end. "Encore, encore."

He takes an exaggerated bow. "Be sure to tip the musician on the way out."

I root around in my wallet for some pennies and toss them at his feet.

He drops to his knees and scoops them up with one hand. "I can eat a cracker! At last, I can eat a cracker, Ma!"

His theatrics make me chuckle.

When he sets down his violin in the case, he glances up at me, earnestness in his brown eyes. "Did it sound okay?"

I beam. "Yes. For something you've been working on for less than twenty-four hours, it sounds great."

"Right, of course. It needs work."

"But you'll get there. It's a fantastic start."

He plops next to me. "Mom, that teacher is cool. I really like him. He texted me some new exercises to work on."

I arch a brow. "He did?"

"Yeah, and they're not boring exercises like the ones my last teacher had me do."

"Not boring is a most excellent way to go."

He pops back up, darts to his room, and emerges a few minutes later wearing a pin-striped jersey and punching the inside of a well-worn baseball glove. "Dad is picking me up in fifteen minutes."

"Right. Baseball game tonight."

Soon enough, Jamison stops by, and father and son take off to see the Bronx Bombers. I dive back into work, burying myself in the design for a travel ad campaign.

As the afternoon starts to fade, my social life, or lack thereof, smacks me in the ass.

I have no kid tonight. I was supposed to be on a date.

I push away from my desk, grab my phone, and call Roxy. When she answers, I ask if she wants to go see a movie or grab a bite to eat.

"I would, but I have a date tonight thanks to Plenty of Chunka Burning Hot Love."

"Is that a new site you're using?"

"Sounds promising, doesn't it?"

"Is that really a dating site?"

She laughs. "Nope. I'm going out with this guy who lives around the block. We kept bumping into each other on the subway, and he finally asked me out."

"Oh, right," I say, remembering her telling me about the train dude. "That's awesome."

"What about you and Guitar Hero? Aren't you supposed to go out with him tonight?"

I sigh heavily. I haven't caught her up since the tragedy of yesterday's bitch-slap from fate. "It turns out he's Kyle's new music teacher."

"Ouch."

"I know."

"That's like soap-level mix-up drama."

"It's like a telenovela, sister. Oh, and there's one other little detail we both failed to pick up on when he played at The Grouchy Owl."

"What's that?" Roxy asks curiously.

"He's Mason Hart, former lead singer and guitarist for the Heartbreakers."

She squeals. Her pitch rises so high I yank the phone away from my ear. "I *loved* them. I still love their music. I was listening to 'Hit the Road' the other day. And 'Love Me Like Crazy' is one of my favorite songs ever."

I make a mental note to search for those songs on Spotify later. "I remember playing them when I was lying on my bed in high school, staring at the ceiling, daydreaming of some guy I crushed on."

"Also," she says, her words tumbling out at the speed of light. "William works with Miles Hart. He mentioned it when he started his firm. He took him on a year or two ago."

My jaw drops as she mentions her brother, a finance guy who recently launched his own wealth management company. "Are you kidding? Don't tell me Ike made the intros."

She laughs. "Ha. I don't think so. William snagged a few high-profile clients when he started. Athletes and celebs. But I still can't believe Mason Hart moonlights in a little local bar. And teaches music. That is so cool. It's like the height of I-do-this-because-I-want-to attitude."

I flash back on my conversation with him yesterday. That's exactly why Campbell does what he does. "It is."

I can hear Roxy moving around her apartment, her heels click-clacking against the floor, her cabinet opening and closing as she's probably putting the finishing touches on her makeup. "But what you did was for the best," she says. "Can you imagine what would happen when he was no longer able to deliver multiple Os? You'd ditch him, but he'd still be coming over to teach 'do re mi fa so la ti do.' Can you say super awkward?"

I slump onto my couch. "Somehow, I don't think he'd suddenly lose that ability."

"But the point is, relationships have a way of not working out," she says, ever the cynic. "Speaking of, I need to skedaddle and see if this date will turn into the next relationship that dies an ugly death."

"Good luck, my pessimistic friend."

"Love ya."

When I hang up, I decide to make the most of my solo time.

I find a Saturday night spinster spin class, exercise my old maid brains out, and douse my sore muscles in a hot shower when I'm done.

By seven, I'm the good kind of exhausted, and I'm

decked out in yoga pants and a tank top. Do I know how to party or what?

I grab my trivia book and read several new chapters. I flip open my laptop and play a few online trivia games. I click over to Netflix and see that Idris is still waiting for me. But Netflix also thinks I should watch Hugh Jackman in *Les Mis*, which reminds me . . .

One text can't hurt.

I grab my phone.

Mackenzie: If we can't go out, can you at least tell me the *Les Mis* story you were going to share?

Campbell: Think you can handle it?

Mackenzie: Now my curiosity is completely piqued.

A minute later, a clip from YouTube appears on my phone. I hit play on a grainy video that's about twenty-five years old. And oh my God, Campbell is the most adorable ten-year-old street urchin I've ever seen as he sings about "Little People."

When I'm done, I call him. "I don't mean this in the same way I admired your teenage *Tiger Beat* face, but you are so freaking adorable on stage singing with the French revolutionaries."

He cracks up. "That's my dirty little secret. I started as a child actor. Now you know why I couldn't tell you who I was when I first met you. You'd have run for the hills."

"Oh, ye of little faith. I think it's completely amazing." I practically bounce with excitement. "Dude, you were in a musical. You're not just a rock star, but you were on the Great White Way. My admiration for you is sky-high now."

He laughs harder. "You're a hoot, Mackadoodle."

"Tell me everything about it. What was the stage like? What were the dressing rooms like? How was Fantine? Was she a total diva? I need to know every detail."

I flop down on the couch as he entertains me with tales of what it was like to work on Broadway when he was ten. I'm smiling and laughing the entire time.

He clears his throat. "Hey, are you just hanging out at home alone?"

"I was supposed to have a date with this completely fascinating and handsome guy but that didn't happen."

"Huh. Funny. I was supposed to have a date with this captivating blonde, but then fate decided to fuck us with a chainsaw."

"You should write a song about that. Fate screwing things with a chainsaw. That would be an awesome song."

"Actually, before you called, I was working on a new song for the Righteous Surfboards."

I sit up higher. "You were? Can I hear it?" My voice rises hopefully.

"It's not ready yet. But would you want to when it's farther along?" He sounds eager to share it with me.

"I'd love to. I really dig your music, Campbell."

"Thank you. I like hearing that, especially since it doesn't really seem like it's your style at all."

"Are you kidding? I loved listening to you guys play. I had such a great time, and it wasn't just because I was thinking about you naked," I say, and there's something that's kind of freeing, I'm learning, about talking to someone I like but can't date. It's as if I can say all these things that I might have held close to the vest before. Knowing it's not going anywhere unleashes the honesty.

"It's good to know my songs can transcend thoughts of nudity."

"It's proof of your musical talent." I lean back against the couch pillows, settling into the conversation. "Where's your daughter tonight?"

"She's playing miniature golf. There's some glow-in-the-dark miniature golf place where she went with a bunch of friends."

"I know that place. It's so fun. Everything is orange and yellow and neon green."

"Wait. You're a superstar at mini golf too?"

I laugh. "I am better at trivia, but I can hold my own in miniature golf."

"It'd be fun to play with you sometime," he says, a little naughty tone to his voice.

"Why would it be fun?"

His voice does that husky, sexy thing I like as he says, "I'm just picturing you swinging a golf club, and I'm thinking about how your ass would look. All nice and tight and just begging me to nibble on it."

Laughing, I shake my head. "Your mind lives in the gutter, Campbell. Literally lives there."

"I have never denied that. I am a complete gutter dweller when it comes to you, and when it comes to you coming."

"There you go again."

"I'm relentless. If we were in the same room, I'd be eating you out and making you come."

"Oh my God! You never stop."

"I know. It's a sickness. The only thing that makes me stop is when your lips are on my cock."

I can't stop laughing. "What am I supposed to do with you? Tell me what you're up to tonight. What are you going to do when we get off the phone?"

"Get off?"

"You win. I throw in the towel."

"Fine. I was going to watch an episode of *The Discovery Prism Show*."

I sit up straighter. "Oh, I've heard of that. It's all about hidden and off-the-beaten-path places to visit around the world."

"Yeah, it's totally cool. I watched the ones on Vienna and Amsterdam. I figured I might tackle Stockholm tonight."

"I've been meaning to see it."

"It's on Netflix."

I slide my laptop closer and log in to the site. "Hey, look at that! It's on my Netflix too."

"Isn't that the darnedest thing? Does your Netflix have the Stockholm one?"

I click through the episodes, feigning shock. "Oh my God. What do you know? It does."

We watch it together. On the phone. Him in Murray Hill, me in the Village, us trying to be good.

We learn about a hidden bathhouse in Stockholm, and a subway station that's practically an art gallery. We check out the episodes on Prague, Tokyo, and also Beijing, commenting as we go, sharing our thoughts, talking about whether we'd visit those places or not.

By the time the night ends, we've done exactly what we weren't supposed to do. We've had a date.

CHAPTER 15

Mackenzie

On Tuesday, Campbell comes over for a lesson. We behave, and we don't let on that we watched Netflix together on Saturday night. I don't flirt with him. I definitely don't make any naughty comments.

When he leaves I walk him to the door, down the hall, and into the foyer where we're alone since I don't live in a doorman building.

"Thank you. Sounded like it was a great lesson," I say, as we near the mailboxes, our footsteps echoing across the tiles.

He drags a hand through those soft, dark locks. "It was a great lesson. I've given Kyle a lot to work on, but he dives right into things. I love his attitude."

"He's a hard worker. He'll absolutely do what you tell him to."

"Good to know," he says, stopping at the door. His eyes travel over my body as if he's cataloging me from head to toe in my skinny jeans and the loose tank top that shows off my ink.

I might have spent some extra time pre-lesson choosing a casual outfit that looks super-hot. The effect seems to be working. I'm such a bad influence on myself.

"You better go," I say, my voice a little throaty as I reach for the door handle.

He nods wisely. "Because you want to jump me here in your foyer?"

I laugh. "Exactly."

"It's a completely mutual desire to engage in foyer-jumping."

"But a desire best left un-acted upon."

"As some desires go."

He takes off, and two days later he's back again because they're doing lessons twice a week.

When I open the door, I brace myself for an onslaught of handsome.

It's really unfair this man has such an abundance of good looks. Surely, somewhere, some guy is begging to be whacked once with the pretty stick Campbell was smacked with more than a few times. Campbell Evans is a stunner, and he's also literally the coolest-looking music teacher in all of Manhattan. Look at him. Those jeans that hug his legs . . . that shirt that shows off his tattoos . . . those motorcycle boots that make me want to hop on the back of a bike and ride away with him . . .

"Do you actually have a motorcycle?" I ask, staring at his shoes before I raise my gaze to meet his eyes.

"Of course," he says, with a wink. "It's a requirement of all musicians to have one."

I key in on the word *have*. "But do you *use* it?"

He scoffs. "Hell no. If I use it, my teenager will think it's okay to date a guy who rides a bike, and it is never, ever okay for my daughter to date someone who rides a bike."

"Clearly."

I let him into my home and excuse myself to the makeshift office area in my bedroom where I dive into my design work. During the hour-long lesson, I pick up on bits and pieces of their conversation. Kyle laughs, and they talk, discussing Beethoven and Mozart. Campbell tells a story about the first Beethoven piece he ever learned to play, and Kyle tells him he started with a rudimentary version of "Ode to Joy."

The violin starts up again, and—no. *Two* violins. Is Campbell playing too? The music soars, and the instrument weeps with happiness as the man I'm crushing on plays it. It's like the violin knows someone who loves it madly is touching its strings, making poetry with a bow. I try to concentrate on my design work, but hearing the two of them attempt the basics of a duet is too distracting. The music they make is hauntingly beautiful—a mix of someone devastatingly talented with someone trying to rise up and reach that level.

"You guys sounded great together. That was gorgeous," I say when the lesson ends.

"I like playing with him," Kyle says earnestly, and I smile, glad he has the chance to learn from someone he admires.

* * *

The next week Kyle is deep into the schoolwork of the fall semester, but he's practically bouncing when Campbell arrives because he wants to show him what he's been working on. When he plays a new piece, Campbell high-fives him then gives him a few pointers. Kyle plays the music again, a little better the second time.

At the end of the lesson, I ask how it went, but I can't get more than a one-word answer—*good*—because they're debating how far the Yankees will go in the post-season. They're discussing outfield prospects and how the manager is doing and if the bullpen can ever truly deliver when it counts.

After that, Campbell hands Kyle some sheet music. "Why don't you work on this Arcade Fire piece for next week?"

Kyle's big brown eyes widen. "They have the coolest violins in their music."

"They do. It's rare to find a rock band that knows how to use the violin, but when you do find one, it's epic."

"Only we don't call it epic. We call it sick," Kyle says with a glint in his eyes.

Campbell shrugs. "I dunno, man. I might still call it epic when those guys go orchestra-style for a rock song."

"For you, I'll make an exception, especially since my string quartet wants to play a mix of rock and classical for a concert we have next month."

"A concert? You've been holding out on me."

I chime in, still excited over Kyle's news, "He just found out about it earlier in the week. His string quartet—he and his friends he plays with—was invited to perform at the community center near us."

Campbell holds a palm up to high-five. "That's sick, and we will make sure you practice hard for it."

Kyle nods. "Tons of practice."

As Campbell heads to the door, I tell Kyle he

needs to get cracking on his math homework before he attempts Arcade Fire.

Kyle groans. "I hate math."

"What kind of math are you working on?" Campbell asks.

"We have a unit on geometry. It's evil," Kyle says with a hiss.

"Need any help? I'm not too shabby at geometry."

"Really?" Kyle's voice rises in excitement.

Campbell looks at the clock above the stove. "Sam's at soccer practice. I have an hour before I need to get her."

"You don't have to," I say softly.

His eyes lock with mine, his irises kind when he says, "It's okay. I want to."

"Let me at least make you something to eat."

"I don't turn down good food."

Campbell sits at the kitchen table to help Kyle with the horror known as geometry, while I make fantastic chicken sandwiches with pesto, homemade artichoke dip, and some sun-dried tomatoes. I wrap them up in napkins and tuck them neatly in Tupperware. I hand them to Campbell in a paper shopping bag when he's finished. "For you and Sam for dinner. As a thank you."

He smiles. "You didn't have to do that."

"You didn't have to help with math."

"I wanted to."

"I wanted to make sandwiches," I say, and after he says goodbye to Kyle, I walk him to the foyer again.

He pauses at the door.

Don't go.

I want him to stay. I want him to make my body sing.

Steering my thoughts from that dangerous territory, I focus on what I can ask—the things I can do to prolong his goodbye. "How did your song go? Did you ever finish writing it?"

"Yeah, I did." He arches a brow skeptically. "Did you really want to hear it?"

"Absolutely." Then I consider his question. "Is there a reason I wouldn't want to hear it?"

He smiles widely and shakes his head. "I'll send it to you tonight."

Before he leaves, I reach out and set my hand on his firm arm. "By the way, I'm glad you're his teacher, Campbell. And I'm glad we've figured out how to be friends," I say, since for the last week we've exchanged a few texts, and we chat at the lessons, but we've been on our best behavior.

He moves in closer and tucks a strand of my hair over my ear. "We might be friends, and you might be the mom of one of my students, but don't think that changes for a second that I'm thinking about how I'd like to peel off those jeans, slide my tongue between your legs, and feel your sweet heat on my lips."

"Oh God," I gasp. My knees wobble. Campbell darts out a hand and clasps my arm to steady me. "You're terrible."

"Am I? Am I truly terrible?"

I shake my head. "You can't resist turning me on."

He whispers, "Are you turned on?"

"So much."

"Good. Then text me when he's asleep, and I'll send you my song."

* * *

Five hours later, I send Campbell a text to tell him I'm ready.

He replies with an MP3 file. I plug in my earbuds and hit play.

The rasp of a guitar fills my ears. It's a hot, sexy sound, like a late summer night, and after a few seconds, his voice joins in, sending a shiver up my spine with the first words he breathes in that growly rasp.

He sings about wanting, about a woman he can't have, about the way she feels soft and tender in his hands, hot against his lips. How she trembles when he whispers to her in the dark, how she moves under him, like water, like air.

Holy shit.

This song is sex.

This song is me.

This song is everything he wants to do to me. I play it again, and again, as I write back.

Mackenzie: Wow. This song is WHITE HOT.

Campbell: It's about you.

Mackenzie: Yeah?

Campbell: Could you tell?

Mackenzie: I was hoping it would be about me.

Campbell: I was hoping it'd turn you on.

Mackenzie: I haven't really been turned off since you left. But I'm turned on higher now.

Campbell: Are you in bed?

Mackenzie: Yes.

Campbell: Where are your hands?

Mackenzie: Where do you want them to be?

Campbell: Inside your panties. Between your legs. Flying across your wetness. If I can't touch you, you ought to touch yourself and imagine it's me fucking you, fingering you, licking you after writing a song about you.

Mackenzie: God, I'm dying. That's the sexiest thing anyone's ever said to me.

Two minutes later, I write back.

Mackenzie: Mmmmm ... you're amazing in my fantasy.

Campbell: Same here.

I go a second time, picturing that man across town with his hand in his briefs, his fist around his cock, getting off to me.

CHAPTER 16

Campbell

I play Mackenzie's song the next night at a new spot in Soho. The crowd likes it, judging from the number of people trying to sing along. Of course, that's a tall order since the tune is new. But they try valiantly to guess at the words and mouth them as we sing, and that's the best sign of all. That's how you know you have a hit on your hands—when the audience does everything possible to sing it right back to you.

When we finish, I wrap my hands tight around the mic. "You guys rock. Thank you so much for coming out on a Thursday night. May your dreams be filled with rock 'n' roll and dirty thoughts, and everything good in the world."

I high-five JJ, while Cade gives me a thumbs-up as we head offstage.

We pack up, riffing on what went well with the show.

"We're starting to draw regular audiences," Cade says. "If you look at our Instagram, we're growing, and people are commenting they're coming to our gigs. Before you know it, they're gonna figure out who you are."

I laugh it off as I set my guitar in its case. "I won't be the first guy who's ever moonlighted."

Cade grabs my shoulder. "And one day you're going to come out, and it'll be astonishingly magnificent. I can't wait to witness that moment."

I roll my eyes as I shrug him off. I look at both of them, shifting gears. "Hey, guys. You know how Miller is talking about trying to get back together?"

JJ laughs. "When is Miller not talking about getting back together?"

"True. It's pretty much his favorite thing to discuss in the entire universe. But I was thinking, remember that band that opened for us a few weeks ago when we played at the Lucky Spot? Female lead singer with jet-black hair and pipes for days?"

JJ nods salaciously. "Oh yeah. Rebecca Crimson, hot as fuck."

"Whatever. It's her voice I'm talking about. It hit me the other night—she had one of those husky, sexy, bourbon voices that could pair perfectly with Miller's."

JJ scratches his bearded jaw. "Yeah, maybe. But if Miller wants to be a Heartbreaker, how is a woman going to help?"

"He's not going to be a Heartbreaker. But this is the one thing he's never really tried before—singing with a woman. He could be fantastic paired up with that smoky, Joss Stone-type sound."

JJ whistles. "Rebecca does sound like Joss. And incidentally, Joss Stone has the hottest voice I've ever heard. If you could fuck a voice, hers would be the one I'd want to bang."

Cade jumps in as he packs up his bass. "Fucking a voice would be like fucking a ghost, I bet."

I stare at him as if he's grown five noses. "Fucking a ghost?"

"Oh yeah," he says, his expression intently serious. "Did you see that chick on Facebook recently who married a ghost pirate? She was talking about the best positions to have sex with him."

I crease my brow, trying to rein in the laughter. "And what are the best positions for sexual relations with a ghost pirate?"

"Obviously, the ghost has to be on top," Cade says matter-of-factly.

"Because otherwise you'll crush it?" JJ asks.

Cade shrugs. "Probably. Sad, huh?"

"Yeah. Anyway, ghost-sex isn't a thing. And screwing a voice isn't a thing either. Sorry to break it to you, J-Man," I say.

"That's okay. Sometimes I just pretend I'm getting it on with Joss Stone."

"And is your wife okay with that?" I ask.

"You think she isn't pretending I'm Justin Timberlake?"

I cackle as I shut my guitar case. "That's her go-to? Of all the singers, you picked him for her hall pass?"

"She picked him!" JJ says indignantly. "That's her choice. She picked JT over Adam Levine and Jared Leto."

Cade drags his hand through his blond surfer locks. "If I were a chick with a hall pass, I'd totally pick Jared Leto."

I hold up my hands. "Why do I even bother having serious conversations with the two of you?"

JJ claps me on the back. "Men are pigs, Campbell. And I bet your bro will have a hard time singing with Rebecca Crimson once he sees how hot she is."

I sigh heavily. "Men and women can work together. Men and women can be friends. Men and women don't have to be stuck in this Neanderthal existence where they only think and breathe sex."

JJ knocks on the side of my skull. "Where is my friend Campbell? What did you do with him?"

I pat my chest. "I'm right here, being rational."

Cade points at me. "No, man. You're being crazy."

As we walk out, JJ clears his throat. "Listen. I know Rebecca's manager. Want me to reach out to him and put out some feelers?"

"That'd be great. Thank you."

"After that, it's up to Miller."

But I have a hunch this might be exactly what Miller needs.

CHAPTER 17

Mackenzie

The next Wednesday I receive an SOS from my son in the middle of the day. It's one of those fantastic messages that only a thirteen-year-old can send. Meaning, it requires a Rosetta Stone to actually decipher it. Sort of like the time he sent me a message that said *onions today* because he needed to pick them up for the Easter food drive.

This one says *Beethoven Sonata*.

I write back and ask for more info.

His reply is speedy, but obscure and blessed with a typo. *Sheer music.*

I fire back. *Sheet music? Which ones?*

He replies *today*, then adds a sorry-faced emoticon along with a begging one.

I ask again which sheet music.

But he doesn't reply, and I suspect he must have stuffed his phone into his backpack to return to class.

Time for me to spring into action. Fortunately, I'm nearly done with a magazine ad for a watchmaker—I was hired to photoshop the model's hand. Now he looks like he has the manliest, but softest, hand in the world.

I save the file, grab my purse and phone, and catch the subway to the music shop where we usually buy our sheet music. The grizzled guy who works there can likely interpret pre-teen hieroglyphics.

No such luck.

The ponytailed dude working today is new, and incredibly precise. He lists about fifty thousand Beethoven sonatas. He tells me there are tons of sheet music options. "This just isn't enough to go on. I want to help you. Trust me, ma'am, I do. But I'd have to relinquish my degree in music if I just willy-nilly plucked sheet music from the shelves. When you don't know much about music, you need to be more specific."

I shoot him a look that says his condescending attitude isn't welcome. "First, you don't have to call me 'ma'am.' I'm younger than you. And two, I don't think you'd need to turn in your degree simply to help me. But I'll figure it out on my own."

I turn away from him and call Campbell, hoping I'm not interrupting him. He answers on the first ring. "Former teen sensation at your service. How may I pleasure you?"

A laugh bursts from my throat. "Campbell, what if my son had called you?"

"One, he doesn't call from your phone. Two, he texts. Three, who else would it be but you? Four, if it wasn't you, I'm not ashamed if the world learned the truth of my second career operating a phone sex line."

"You are the biggest troublemaker I've ever known, and I'm trying to pick up the sheet music Kyle needs for the next lesson with you. I didn't want to trouble you, but Kyle's note didn't have enough details."

"Oh yeah, I gave him some complicated stuff. You need help?"

"Like pasta needs sauce."

"Where are you?"

I tell him the name of the music store.

"I'm three blocks away. Stay there. Don't move. I'm coming to your rescue, m'lady."

"I'm not helpless," I tell him, but I kind of am right now, considering Ponytail's disdain for me.

"Let me believe you are. There is something

rather sexy about you standing in a music store needing my assistance."

Five minutes later, the bell above the door chimes and in strides a guitar god. Campbell walks toward me, wearing faded blue jeans that hug his strong thighs and a form-fitting T-shirt that manages to show off his flat abs and toned arms.

Ponytail stares at him slack-jawed. No words come out of his open mouth, just a lip sync of *oh my God*.

Campbell nods to the man and says, "How you doing?"

Ponytail squeaks.

When Campbell arrives by my side, he gives a cocky grin and says, "You're looking at me like I'm the answer to all your prayers."

"How do you do that?"

He flashes a too-debonair smile. "How do I exude rugged charm every single second of the day? It is quite a talent, isn't it?"

I point to his midsection. "No. How do you have such flat abs?"

"Ah, you like my abs?"

"Yes. Is it not obvious?"

He scratches his jaw. "I don't recall your hands on my belly enough to know if it's obvious. Show me." He gestures to his stomach.

I laugh. "Not here in the store."

He leans in close as we stand in the aisle amid the drum music. "I won't count it against you."

"Count it against me in what?"

"In your efforts to be a good girl. I feel this would be a worthwhile exception to your good-girl pursuits."

One little touch won't change the score. I drag my nails down his stomach, and I nearly howl in pleasure.

Campbell groans in a delicious voice that sends sparks dancing up and down my spine. "Well, that's not fair. You rendered me helpless after I arrived to rescue you."

"Rescue me, then," I tell him.

He tips his chin to the violin music, and without batting an eye, he snatches the music for several violin sonatas, rattling off the names as he plucks each one from the shelf. Once I purchase the music, we head to the street. "Thanks again. I guess I should go."

He tilts his head to the side, his playful eyes sparkling. "Or we could get a cup of coffee, since we sort of happened to run into each other in the middle of the day."

"It was quite happenstance, wasn't it?"

"Completely. I know the guy who runs the shop next door."

"Happenstance coffee next door sounds great."

After all, we're friends. We like each other's company. There's no reason not to have a cup of joe.

We turn into Dr. Insomnia's Tea and Coffee Emporium. Campbell knocks fists with the tall guy behind the counter. "Hey, Tommy. What'll it take to get a coffee in this joint?"

The guy breathes out hard. "Don't know. That's a tough one."

Campbell asks what I'd like, then places our order and guides me to a table near the back. "Let me grab our drinks."

He makes small talk at the counter with his friend then joins me a minute later, drinks in hand. "Tell me more about Mackadoodle."

I laugh and take a drink. "What do you want to know?"

"Any sisters or brothers?"

"I have one sister. Jackie lives in Connecticut and has three little kids, all under the age of five. We were close growing up."

"Are you still?"

"For the most part. I try to get out there often and see her—and my parents, since they live there too."

"What did you and Jackie like to do when you were kids?"

"I loved to read to her. She was kind of a scaredy-cat, so I broke her down and trained her to like *Goosebumps*."

"You trained her?" He arches his brow as he drinks his coffee.

"Of course." I square my shoulders proudly. "No sister of mine was going to be a sissy. I taught her she could handle creepy ventriloquist villains and scary talking cars. And when I wasn't toughening her up, we pretended we were rock stars."

He smiles widely. "Did you play an instrument?"

I shake my head. "I shredded a most amazing air guitar, and she pounded away on a fantastic set of mime drums."

"Excellent. I see you hit all the basic requirements for growing up."

"Pretending to be in a band is definitely one of them. Sort of like having a treehouse. Did you and your brothers have a treehouse?"

"Yes, and we played music in it."

I laugh, loving that image. "That's brilliant. I can see that."

"We're pretty close now too, like you and your sister." He drums his fingers on the table. "Three kids. That's a handful."

"Yes, indeed. But Jackie's happiest when she's up to her elbows in mac and cheese and Legos."

"What about you?"

"I do love mac and cheese too."

He smiles. "Do you wish you had any more kids like Jackie does?"

I arch a brow. "This really is a deep-dive conversation."

"I'm making the most of my happenstance coffee."

He is indeed. In fact, I like that about Campbell. He doesn't waste time or words. He grabs hold of opportunities, like he did the first night with me, like asking for the chance for a second date, and then at Jamison's house when he grabbed the opportunity to get to know me more. He seems to sink his teeth into life's moments and savor them when they come around.

I meet his gaze, my tone serious. "Is that because of what happened to you? Losing Sam's mom? Is that why you grab these moments and make the most of them?"

He cocks his head to the side as if considering that for the first time. "That's a good point. I hadn't thought of it like that, but yeah, maybe it is. I try not to waste time doing pointless shit. I want to savor every moment." He gestures to me. "And that means I want to understand this fascinating woman I like spending random moments with. So, back to you. More kids—yay or nay?"

"Ah, my turn again. And I've thought about it—more kids. But it's not in the cards. And that's okay. Besides, I can't imagine starting over again now. Can you?"

He scoffs, shaking his head adamantly. "No way. I feel like I'm the astronaut who made it around the moon and now I'm circling home. Almost done, you know?"

"We're nearly in the homestretch. I honestly have to laugh sometimes when I hear from my mom friends with toddlers and babies. They're up to their arms in diapers and have kids with their fingers reaching for sockets. Don't you feel like you've earned your badge?"

"I have my war wounds. That's not to say that having a teenager is easy. I really do think the teen years are my favorite though. That might sound crazy, but there's something nice about being able to discuss the state of the world, or politics, or the environment, or right or wrong, or bullying with your kid, know what I mean?"

"Yes, and when they suddenly like to talk about other things besides toy trucks or princess dresses, you can make an impact in a brand-new way."

"Precisely."

As we drain our coffees, we chat more about the ups and downs of parenthood, favorite games we played as kids, and whether we're close with our families. I learn Sam visits with Campbell's mom and dad once a month in Jersey and always has, and Campbell relishes that closeness she has with her grandparents. I tell him that Kyle is tight with my parents and my sister. Neither of us says it aloud, but I suspect we're both secretly delighted we're similar in how we've raised our kids. It's a bond I never sought to have with a man, yet it's one I like a lot.

"Hey, Mackadoodle," he says, holding up his empty mug.

"Yeah?"

He leans forward, his eyes holding mine. My stomach flips. "I like talking to you."

I smile like a giddy woman who really likes a guy. As way more than a friend. "I like talking to you too."

He stands up and moves to the same side of the table as me, wrapping his arm around the back of my chair, leaning in close. "I like looking at your mouth."

I shiver. "You do?"

"Your lips are so fucking sexy. I know you think I'm a filthy bastard."

"I don't think that," I whisper. I lower my head, my bangs falling over my forehead.

He brushes them away. "Did I embarrass you?"

I shake my head. "No, it's just you're doing it again."

"What am I doing?" he asks, but he has to know. The sexy smirk tells me he does.

"You're turning me on when you're not supposed to."

He groans and brushes strands of hair off my

shoulder. I tremble from his touch. "You get turned on when I tell you how sexy your lips are?"

I nod as pleasure lights up my skin.

"Do you get turned on when I flirt with you?"

"All. The. Time."

He grins. "What else turns you on?"

A part of me is keenly aware I'm playing with fire. This kind of flirting is dangerous. It threatens the stable, comfortable life I've carved out—one that now includes Campbell as a regular fixture in it.

But the fire feels so good. It draws me in and heats me up. I want to feel the flame, so I nibble on my lip. "Sometimes, when you're at my house and I walk past you while you're teaching my son, I swear butterflies launch a full-scale attack in my belly, and I'm thinking filthy thoughts, and kissing thoughts, and crazy thoughts, and it's all a mess."

Something like a growl comes from his throat. "Kind of a mess for me too. And sometimes I want to make a mess of your hair." He drags a hand up the back of my neck, and I tremble. Then I gasp as he tugs on a chunk of my hair. "Would you think I was a dirty bastard if I told you I was rock-hard right now?"

I purse my lips and shake my head. "Would you think I was dirty if I tried to cop a feel?"

"Fuck no."

I've zoomed past restraint, because the next thing I know my exploring hand slides along his thigh, inching up to his crotch. I'm feeling him up underneath the table, stroking the hard outline of his erection through his jeans. In this moment, I don't care about good-girl pursuits and what counts and doesn't count. The only thing that counts is this fire that needs to be quenched.

"Love the way you feel," I tell him.

He groans, low and carnal, and brings his lips to my ear. "Time for that rain check?"

CHAPTER 18

Campbell

You know those commercials where the guy is out on the golf range, and he's just hit a fabulous shot? Or where the dude is proudly sailing the seven seas as skipper of his own rig? And the ads say: *This is my happy place*?

Those guys have nothing on me.

Right here. Happy place.

My buddy Tommy letting me pop into the tiny office at the back of his coffee shop for a midday blow job—that's cause for jumping for joy. Not that I told him explicitly what was going to go down. I just said, "Do me a solid and let me check out your office for ten minutes."

Mackenzie's hands are speed demons as she unzips my jeans and pushes down my briefs. My cock greets her with a full-on salute.

"Nice to see you too," she murmurs, staring at my dick.

"I bet the view's even better from your knees."

"Smart-ass."

I set my hands on her shoulders. "Allow me to help you."

I guide her to the floor. I'm so fucking grateful we're abandoning the we-don't-want-to-screw-each-other-senseless act, at least for the moment. "I'd like to make a mess of your hair, and now your lipstick."

She flashes a grin as she wraps a hand around my shaft, her touch sending jolts of electricity through me. "Let's see what we can do about that." She flicks her tongue over the tip, pure desire flashing across her brown eyes as she strokes and licks.

"That's a beautiful view."

"How's this?" She presses her cheek against my shaft.

I shudder. It's filthy and reverent at the same time. She rubs me against the side of her face, and holy fucking hell. My dick looks good against her soft skin.

She moans and whispers as she rubs, and I could die right now. She is so fucking sexy like this. Especially when she slaps my dick lightly against her face. *Dear Lord.*

"Do it again," I tell her, and she obliges, and I'm nearly burned alive with lust.

Like my dirtiest prayers have been answered, she drags my cock to her soft, warm lips and draws me in an inch. I growl in incomprehensible pleasure as her mouth engulfs the tip.

"Yeah, just like that," I mutter as she swirls her tongue across the head.

She lifts her hooded eyes up to me as she sucks. She's going to tease me, toy with me. My legs are shaking with desire, my muscles strung tight with wanting. "Don't," I warn.

"Don't what?"

"Don't tease me, Sunshine."

Her eyes twinkle with naughtiness. Laughing, she peppers kisses on the side of my shaft. I curl my hands around her head, gripping her skull. "That's not what I need, and you know it."

She smiles with the head of my dick in her mouth. "It's not?" she mumbles.

I shake my head. "Get your lips all the way around me."

She flicks her tongue along my length, licking her way up and down, teasing me as if it's her favorite thing to do. Sliding her hand between my legs, she cups my balls, fondling. I shudder as she runs her nails across them. It's like she's delivering an electric charge to every single cell in my body. I'm lit up. I'm on fire.

"Please," I groan.

"Please what?"

"Please suck me hard."

She wiggles her eyebrows and dives in. All the way. She goes from zero to sixty in two seconds. "That's it, Sunshine. That's fucking it. Suck me so hard your cheeks hurt."

My dick hits the back of her throat, and somewhere birds sing. The heavens open. A comet streaks across the sky.

Wrapping my hands tighter around her head, I fuck and fuck. "This is my happy place," I mutter as my dick slides in and out of her mouth. Her pink lips are so tight, her eyes so fierce. Her attention is a thing of beauty.

The friction in her mouth is astonishing, and she sucks with such abandon, such determination I can barely take it. Pleasure sizzles up and down my spine. Fucking bliss takes over, throwing me into a tailspin of ecstatic oblivion.

I go up in flames as I fuck her mouth, shuddering as I reach the edge. "Fuck, Sunshine. Gonna come so hard down your throat."

My vision blurs as white-hot pleasure speeds through me, and waves of desire tug me under, toppling over me. I moan her name as I come undone.

A minute later, I yank her up and kiss her hard, pushing her hair away from her face. "I can now die having had the greatest blow job in the history of the world."

"Good. Write a song about it, please."

I glance over at the desk, hungry to have her, to bury my mouth between her legs. "Why don't you get on that desk and spread your legs?"

She shakes her head. "No way. We're supposed to be good."

I blink. "That didn't stop us a minute ago."

She pats my hip. "It doesn't count. Don't you know?"

I furrow my brow. Perhaps the orgasm has robbed me of brain cells. "Why doesn't my dick in your mouth count?"

"That was a continuation of the one-night stand. So it's like an addendum to an existing incident. It doesn't break my commitment to be good." Her expression is full of laughter, but there's a touch of seriousness in her eyes, and it tells me she's been thinking, trying to make sense of what happened between us.

"It doesn't break your resolve because it's not new canoodling?" I ask, since I want to understand her logic too, such as it is.

She shakes her head. "Trust me, I've been working this through in my head. It's definitely not a new instance. Since I had always planned to give you a fantastic blow job, I was simply finishing the work I started a few weeks ago, and the canoodling moratorium remains." Her voice is no-nonsense, reasoned to the core. "Now, if I tried to do something like give you a hand job, that would count as a new canoodle and would therefore be a violation. But as it stands, we're still in the clear."

I laugh, shaking my head. "I don't like your rules because I want to taste you right now, but if you'd like to pretend my dick accidentally fell in your mouth, so be it."

She rises on her tiptoes and plants a kiss on my lips. "If I could find a way to accidentally slip onto your tongue, believe me, I would."

I'll be praying for that happy accident to occur.

* * *

A little later, I head to Mackenzie's for the lesson with Kyle, and I put blinders on so I don't let on that my student's mom . . .

Nope. Won't go there. Won't even think dirty thoughts while I'm teaching.

I am Super Music Teacher, 100 percent focused

on these sonatas and on saying a chaste goodbye to both student and parent.

When I return to my apartment that evening, I'm overwhelmed by the scent of salted caramel, and my ears are treated to loud pop music blasting from every speaker in the apartment's sound system.

My brother and my daughter are singing in the kitchen, using spatulas for mics and dancing in their aprons, skulls for Sam and rainbow-breathing unicorns for Miller.

"Guys! I have neighbors! You can't play it that loud."

I turn down the volume, but that doesn't stop my brother from belting out a pop tune about needing love. Samantha finishes the chorus at the top of her powerful lungs, hitting all the notes because my kid has a helluva set of pipes on her. Then she licks caramel off the end of the spatula and waves at me. "Hi, Dad. Miller came over to help me bake."

Miller winks at her. "You can call it baking, but you know it was really performing magical artistry in the kitchen."

"They're salted caramel brownie bars, Dad." Samantha points to a baking sheet on the counter. "And they're definitely the best."

I arch a brow, waiting for her to say they're the worst too. But she doesn't. Apparently, when she cooks with Miller everything is simply the best.

Miller has that effect on people—he's a dose of positivity. In a bad mood? Take a Miller pill. Bummed over the state of the world? Spend an hour with Miller and everything will be sunshine and unicorns again.

"Hey, Campbell," Miller says, draping an arm around Sam. "Did you hear us rocking that duet?"

"Um, did you think I missed it?"

"And doesn't Sam sing the shit out of a song?"

"Language, Miller."

"Dad," my daughter chides, "I've heard a lot worse."

"But you don't need to hear it in my house."

"Anyway," Miller says, claiming the figurative mic again, "you don't mind if Sam joins a band with me, do you? We could be the Rocking Utensils."

"By all means, I'd have no problem letting my fourteen-year-old sing with you—and tour the world too."

Miller pumps a fist and Sam laughs as she slides brownies off the tray and onto a plate.

"But speaking of singing with a woman, what do you think about the gal I mentioned the other night?" I ask.

Miller emits an approving noise. "Rebecca is good. We could make beautiful music together."

Samantha furrows her brow. "If you're going to sing with a woman, why don't you do it with Ally?"

she asks, mentioning his longtime best friend, who's also a once-upon-a-time singer. She dominated on YouTube for a few years with her brother, raking in millions of views with their clever mash-ups.

"Ally?" Miller asks, as if Samantha suggested he take up unicycling while learning Romanian in the rain.

"Ally," I repeat. "The woman you hang out with all the time. Brunette? About this tall?" I hold my hand above my shoulder.

Miller smacks his forehead. "Oh, thanks. I didn't know who you meant otherwise."

"Miller, she's the best. It's like listening to angels when she sings," Samantha says, staring at him as if he's gone mad for not getting this.

I chime in, "And it's shocking you've never considered that since you've been friends with Ally forever." I grab a stool and park myself across from them at the counter, waiting for Miller to tell me what he thinks of either Ally or the Joss Stone sing-alike. "What do you think, Mill?"

Miller scratches his jaw. "You know things don't always go my way when I play with someone I'm friends with. It's caused all sorts of trouble in the past."

I scoff. "Ally is hardly a troublemaker."

"Yeah, but that's not the issue."

"What's the issue, Uncle Miller?"

He heaves a sigh. "Friendship and music don't always mix."

Sam pats him on the shoulder. "It's sweet you care so much about her."

He glances at me, meeting my eyes. "But the real issue is I'm still so wounded you won't get back together with me. Sam thinks it's a good idea if we sing again, don't you?"

My daughter tsks him. "Do not get me into trouble with my dad."

"You could never get in trouble. You're the apple of his eye," Miller says.

"She is the apple of my eye, but she can also get in trouble, especially if she hangs out with you, troublemaker."

Miller waggles his eyebrows, owning it.

I snag a brownie from the tray and take a bite. I moan in appreciation. "This is divine."

Sam smiles. "Speaking of divine, I want to get the recipe for those sandwiches you brought home the other night. The sauce was to die for. Can you ask that woman what it was made of?"

I smile, loving that I have a legit reason to text Mackenzie. "I can."

Miller arches a brow. "One of your student's moms is making you sandwiches? I smell a crush." He points at me, like a kid singing the kissing-in-a-tree tune. "Someone has a crush on Mason Hart."

"Eww, gross," Samantha says.

I roll my eyes because Miller is flirting far too close to the truth, and I need to divert his attention. "So, would Ally sing with you?"

He slinks around the counter and punches my arm, undeterred. "Who is she? Come on. Fess up. Who's the sandwich-maker?"

"No one," I mumble.

Just the woman who had her lips wrapped around me like a Hoover earlier today. The woman I can't resist flirting with. The woman I love talking to.

Miller turns to Sam with a look of exaggerated shock. "No one? Did you hear that, Sam? You really think she's no one?"

"I wonder if this no one would like a salted caramel brownie," Sam says playfully. "Want to bring her some next time you see her?"

I nod. "She'd love that."

Sam points at me. "Busted. She's *so* someone."

That's the trouble. Even as we do our best to avoid entanglements, Mackenzie is quickly becoming someone special.

Or maybe it's because we're doing our worst.

CHAPTER 19

Mackenzie

"And that's how you deal with a trapezoid." Campbell stabs the graph worksheet with the tip of a pencil. "Done!"

Kyle sighs in relief, dragging a hand through his hair. "Trapezoids are the worst."

"Not true," Campbell says, his expression stony. "Rhombuses are the worst."

"Can we agree they're all the worst?"

"Wait till you get to calculus. Everything is awful then," I say from my spot in the kitchen where I'm whipping up my most excellent mac and cheese, complete with gouda and English snap peas.

Campbell stretches his arms, parking them

behind his head. "I beg to disagree. I thought calculus was quite fun."

I shoot him a look then turn to Kyle. "Can you grab the thermometer from the medicine cupboard? Clearly Campbell has a temperature if he thinks calculus was fun."

Kyle laughs. "I think the aliens have taken him over."

"Calculus is neat and orderly. It makes sense. It follows logic. It's not that different from music."

"How the heck are you good at classical music, rock music, and math? That's insanely unfair," I point out as I stir the melted gouda into the glass mixing bowl. Somehow, we've fallen into a routine of music, help with math, and food. It's been a week since our happenstance coffee, and nothing has happened to fall into my mouth again. Shame, that.

But it's for the best. Kyle is flourishing in violin, and I don't want to mess that up.

Campbell leans back in his chair and glances at me. "By the same token, how are you good at trivia, graphic design, and parenting?"

I can't help but smile, even as I roll my eyes. "Roxy and I did win at a trivia contest earlier this week. We're trying out another pub that has trivia, so Ike doesn't kick us out of The Grouchy Owl for winning all the time," I add, with a wink.

"You rock, Mom," Kyle says.

"And how is Kyle good at music, and basketball, and history?" Campbell posits.

Kyle gives a self-deprecating snort. "I'm not that good at basketball."

"Work with me, buddy," Campbell says to my son.

"Okay, I'm good at knowing details about sports stars. How's that?"

Campbell high-fives him. "There you go. Anyway, calculus goes hand in hand with music. Every piece of music is a function. Music works in intervals and ratios just like calculus."

Kyle tilts his head as if considering Campbell's words. "And reading music is like reading math symbols?"

Campbell's eyes light up. "Yes, like a treble or bass clef. And each measure is divided into beats, and the time signatures are usually written as a fraction."

Kyle grabs some sheet music on the table and studies it. "Dude. You're right."

"A lot of times musicians are better than average at solving more complex mathematical equations," Campbell adds. "Want to know why?"

Kyle's smile brightens. "Why?"

Campbell taps the side of Kyle's head. "Because you're trained for detail. For discipline. Because you practice until you're perfect. All of that carries into solving math problems."

"If I want to improve my ability to balance my checkbook, should I listen to Mozart?" I chime in, and Campbell laughs.

"It's not a bad idea."

"I'm kidding. I'm a wiz at balancing my checkbook. Math is hard, but it's important. If you're naturally good at it, even better. But even if you're not, you still need to learn it," I tell my son.

"Totally, Mom. Also, I'm super hungry. Is that ready?"

"It is, and it's delicious. Campbell, want some?"

He pats his belly. "I'm not sure I could live with myself if I turned it down."

* * *

When we're done with dinner, I scoop up some leftovers for Campbell's daughter. He snaps his fingers. "She was asking for your sandwich sauce recipe the other week."

"Is that so?"

He presses his hands together in a plea. "Any chance you'd share it?"

"For her? Of course."

I grab a sheet of paper from a notebook and jot

down the details, adding a doodle of a girl in an apron at the end of the paper.

"She's going to love that," Campbell says, as I tuck the goodies into a bag and hand it to him.

After he says goodbye to Kyle, I walk him to the foyer.

"So..." he says.

"So..."

"We've been good."

This is the third time I've seen him since the coffee shop encounter. "No accidental slips of the tongue."

"I think we deserve medals." He leans in to drop a kiss on my cheek. "Especially since I still want to get my lips all over you. Everywhere."

I want that too.

More and more, every day I spend with him.

I want the laughter and the naughtiness. I want the dinners and the desserts.

But I also want what's best for my son.

I've had enough detours in life. I've had to improvise in my career and with my plans. I've had to turn onto new roads to reach my destination. That's why I need to be careful, so I say goodbye. Chastely.

Later that night, Campbell texts me a video of his daughter.

She's eating a spoonful of the mac and cheese

and rolling her eyes in pleasure. "Oh my God, this is the greatest mac and cheese ever, and you are literally the best cook in the world. You have an open invitation to come on my baking show anytime you want."

* * *

Mackenzie: I love your show! I just watched a ton of segments. It would be an honor to be on it.

Samantha: The honor is all mine! Your food is the BEST! I LOVE HAVING GUEST COOKS ON MY SHOW!

Mackenzie: I can't wait. Do I need to bring anything?

Samantha: JUST AN AMAZING RECIPE!

Mackenzie: Fortunately, that's my specialty. :)

* * *

"Just be natural."

    I can do that. I can totally do that.

I smooth my hands down the front of my apron as Samantha smiles into the phone perched in its holder on the stunning kitchen counter.

"Hey, everybody! I have a fabulous special guest today! I cannot believe she agreed to do my show." She stops and squeezes my shoulder. "This woman, who makes the best savory treats in all of Manhattan, is here with me. Can you give Mackenzie a big baker welcome?"

Samantha gestures to me, and I wave to the camera. "Hey, everybody."

"Wait till you try some of her treats. You will die. Just die. Legit die one hundred percent from the awesome." Samantha turns to me. "What yumminess will we make today?"

I flash her an easy grin. "What would you say to baked savory cream cheese and herb donuts?"

Her green eyes widen to saucers. "I'd say that sounds *famazing*."

We get to work on the mixing and the measuring and the baking, with Samantha taking breaks to turn on and off the record button.

At one point when it's off and we're stirring, she says, "How did you learn to be such a great cook?"

"I don't think I'm such a great cook."

"Oh, *stahp*. You are. You're incredible. Everything my dad's brought home has been delicious. Tell me your secret because I want to be a baker someday.

Well, if I'm not a baker, then I want to be superstar ski jumper."

"You ski?"

She shakes her head, her looped-over blonde ponytail brushing her cheeks. "No, but I want to. I think it would be so cool. So would skateboarding."

"So you're going to take up ski jumping at age fourteen in case you want to be one?" I ask, laughing lightly.

"Bad idea?"

"I think you can do whatever you want."

"I wish I could draw like you. I loved your doodle of me. If I could get a tattoo, I totally would."

"What would you have done?"

She stops mixing and stares at the ceiling. "Mountains on one elbow, waves on the other."

"I love that. Any particular reason?"

She returns to the mixing bowl. "Just life's balance, you know? It's a good reminder to climb the mountains and relax on the beach."

I smile. "Good mantra. I like that, and I know what you mean."

She nudges my elbow. "Tell me your cooking secret. How are you so good at it?

I narrow my *eyes*, oh so serious. "You really want to know?"

"Yes, I'm dying," she says as she doles out cheesy donut mix on a tray.

I point to the donut mix. "Cooking is like doodling. You have to try it out. Test things. See what works. I was never afraid to try something with a pen and paper, and I'm the same in the kitchen. I doodled with food till I got it right."

"I love that. We can call this episode Doodling with Mackenzie."

An hour later, she bites into a savory herb donut, and tells me she wants to become a master kitchen doodler.

That is, after she becomes a skater.

* * *

Three days later, Kyle races through his time with Campbell. He rushes out the door the second the lesson is over because Jamison is back in town, waiting in a Lyft to take him to Madison Square Garden to see the Knicks.

I wave goodbye and turn back into my apartment, expecting to see Campbell on the way out. Instead he's waiting for me in the kitchen.

"What's up?" I ask curiously.

"Come here."

I step closer, and he reaches for the waistband of my jeans. Gooseflesh rises on my arms. "We shouldn't do this."

"I know, but I can't help myself. Especially after

that video you did with my daughter," he says, his eyes never straying from mine.

"You liked it?"

He tugs me closer, lining up my pelvis with his. "It was the sexiest thing I've ever seen."

"Oh, please."

"I mean it, Mackadoodle. You helping my kid bake? Holy fuck. So fucking sexy, the way you are with my girl." He leans into my neck and presses a kiss to my skin. "So fucking hot." He drags his stubbled chin along the column of my throat, making me tremble.

"That was hot?"

He growls a *yes*. "I can't resist you. I know you want me to stay away, but it's fucking hard, Sunshine."

"It's hard for me too," I whisper, relieved to admit the patently obvious.

He pulls back and cups my cheeks. "What if we set up rules? What if we agree that sometimes I want you too much to hold back?"

I love that he wants me that way. "You do?"

"You're so sexy, and so fun, and so kind, and I can barely take wanting you this much. Tell me it's the same for you."

His voice is so desperately sexy it melts me. "Don't you know I want you that way too?"

He groans, tugging me closer. "Bend for me,

Sunshine," he whispers in my ear, while grinding his erection against me. "Bend for *us* so we can have each other again. We'll just have rules."

I let out a long sigh, the kind that says I'm relenting. Because I'm terrible at resisting. "Like no dating?"

He nods.

I nibble on the corner of my lips. "No sex with kids in the house?"

"Obviously."

"One last thing. We keep it a secret?"

He answers instantly, "Of course."

I don't think anymore. I don't contemplate detours and unexpected paths. I stop worrying about being good all the time. Maybe I was never that good anyway.

For now, I make a choice based on the way I feel, the way I want. I grab his face. "Fuck me, Campbell."

CHAPTER 20

Campbell

On the one hand, I could set a world record for how fast I strip her to nothing.

On the other, I want to savor every inch of her delicious body.

On the third hand, the clock's ticking, and I'm not getting any younger.

I toss Mackenzie over my shoulder and carry her to her bedroom, fireman-style. "Love your kitchen, and the ambiance it sets for a good, old-fashioned screw is top-notch, but I have a plan for you and your bed."

"Does it involve tying me to the headboard?" she asks, craning her neck to look up at me.

I stop in the doorway and stare at her. "That something you'd like, Sunshine?"

She wiggles her eyebrows. "Maybe you will find out sometime."

I swat her ass. "Maybe I will, now that you've thrown down that little nugget. But first things first." I toss her on the bed, and she yelps as she bounces. With lightning speed, I unzip her jeans and tug them down her legs. She wriggles and pushes her panties down too, and in mere seconds, she's down to nothing on her bottom half.

"Fuck, I've missed this gorgeous view." My eyes are starving, and I gobble up the sight of her strong legs, lovely thighs, and the perfect paradise between them that I haven't spent nearly enough time visiting. It's been almost two months since our night together, and I can barely stand how much I want her. It hurts. It's a physical ache, this desire.

Grabbing her ankles, I yank her down to the end of the bed, her ass at the edge. She squeals, and I fucking love how she laughs. How she finds fun in so many moments. As I slide my hands up her calves, her laughter fades, then it blends into a beautifully needy moan as I reach her thighs and spread them.

She moves with me, letting her legs fall open. My mouth waters as I stare at the gorgeous sight in front of me. She's glistening for me, so fucking wet already.

I turn my face to the inside of her legs and rub my jaw along the soft skin.

Her hands shoot into my hair, and she grabs at my head. "Don't tease me. You've made me wait so long."

I laugh as I rub my sandpaper stubble against her other thigh. "I made you wait, Sunshine? It was me torturing you?"

She kicks her feet against the bed. "Yes. You torture me by being so hot and sweet and interesting, and by writing me songs and being terrific at teaching—"

I put us both out of our misery by dropping my face between her legs.

Hello, sweetness. You taste fantastic.

Her desire floods my tongue. Her liquid heat meets my lips.

She widens her legs even more, spreading completely for me.

That move makes my whole body hum with rampant lust. Her need for this physical connection makes me harder than I've been before. I could lose my mind for her.

I lick and suck where she wants me most. Moaning and panting, she writhes against my face. But I want more of her. I want to be covered in her.

I stop, hop on the bed on my back, and yank her

on top of me. "Sit on my face, Sunshine. I want to be buried in your sweetness."

Her eyes widen in shock, but it's a filthy kind of delighted surprise, since she doesn't protest. She simply climbs on my face and lowers herself on me.

"Yes," I groan as I lick her, while digging my fingers into the flesh of her ass and moving her across my lips.

She slams her palms onto the headboard and goes to town, giving my face a lap dance of the dirtiest variety possible. She's so fucking sexy, chasing her pleasure, knowing what she needs, using my mouth to get what she wants.

She leans her head back, her blonde hair spilling over her shoulders. I stare at the gorgeous column of her throat while I lick her. She likes it rough and greedy, and that suits me fine. I want to consume her, want to devour every delicious drop of her arousal, want to feel her coming all over my face.

Judging from the sounds she's making, that'll be happening any second.

Oh God.

Yes.

Oh my fucking God.

So close, I'm so close, I'm so close.

She's flying, screaming, shouting as she finds her release. She shudders against me, groaning incoherent noises at the top of her lungs. I'm covered in her pleasure, and I couldn't be happier to have Mackenzie flooding my tongue.

A few more moans. A couple of heady pants. An *oh my God, that was incredible*, and she moves off me, coming down from her high.

I kiss her neck. She shivers as my lips dust her skin. "Campbell," she murmurs, and it sounds lush and lingering on her lips.

"Want another?"

She laughs then meets my gaze. "I want you inside me."

"It's like you can read my mind."

I get off the bed. She props herself up on her elbows, looking sexy as hell, wearing a long-sleeved royal-blue shirt and nothing else. "I want to watch you get undressed."

"Same here. Take off your shirt. I want you completely naked," I say as I undo my jeans. I was never terribly good at resisting her, but in hindsight, now that I've had her again, I don't think I stood a chance.

She sits up and strips off her shirt and bra, and I groan as I stare at her nudity. Her tits are beautiful teardrops, and her body is all mine to enjoy. I strip off my Henley, grab a condom from my wallet, and climb between her legs, kneeling.

"Hurry, hurry," she says, as if she's cheering me on.

I shake my head. "Don't want to mess up this part, little Miss Fertile."

"Ohh, good point. By all means, take all the time in the world."

"I thought you might agree with me there." I slide on the condom and rub the head of my dick against her wet folds. She sinks back down on her pillows and moans loudly, a welcoming sound. "I'm so turned on," she whispers, as if it's naughty confession time.

"Good. I like you turned on. Let's keep you this way."

She raises her arms to my chest and loops her hands around my neck. I push into her, sinking into her heat.

"Oh God," she whispers as I bury myself in her.

"So hot. So fucking wet."

"I told you I'm turned on."

"I love it," I murmur as I fill her completely. "I fucking love all this wetness."

Lust takes hold of every inch of my body. It's fantastic to be buried inside her like this. I move in her, and the two of us waste no time finding a rhythm. We're not slow fuckers; we don't seem to like to linger. Mackenzie lifts her hips quickly, planting her feet so she can move with me, grind up into me.

She drags her nails along my back, digging them in. "Harder."

"Woman, I'm doing my best to fuck you hard."

She brings her mouth to my ear. "Hard. Fast. Rough. That's how I like it."

Groaning, I rasp out, "You're fucking perfect, Sunshine." I do as I'm asked, fucking her ruthlessly hard, grabbing her right leg and pushing her thigh up, so she's wide open for me. "Like that?"

"Oh God, yes," she says, moaning, and I drive into her, giving it to her the way she wants—relentlessly.

"Touch yourself," I tell her.

She slides a hand between us, down her stomach, and rubs her clit as I push in and out of her. Her mouth falls open in a gorgeous O.

"You rubbing your sweet pussy. That's so fucking hot. So fucking sexy how you touch yourself. Makes me want to watch you come again and again."

She throws her head back and moans my name, and it turns into a warning bell, since a few strokes are all she needs to send herself tumbling over the edge again.

Once she's there, I'm tempted to put her on her hands and knees and pound into her, but when I stare down at her face, all blissed out and beautiful, I don't want to fuck her from behind.

I don't even want to fuck her hard.

I want to look at her.

Watch her.

Catalog every expression on her face.

I slow my pace, and lower myself to my elbows, and whisper, "Hi."

"Hey," she says, all sexy and smoky.

"Love the way you come," I whisper as I rock slowly, taking my time now, swiveling my hips and finding a luxurious pace.

"I think you're pretty damn good at getting me there. But what about you?"

"Don't worry about me." I bury my face in her neck, and layer kisses on the smooth, soft skin.

"Mmm," she murmurs and reaches her arms around me again, tugging me closer so our chests are pressed together. "This feels so good."

"I know."

It feels fucking amazing.

It feels like I took a different turn down the road. Like we started with raw heat, and we sped through rough-and-fast land, and now we've veered someplace else entirely. We're driving down a new road, and this one's a little more dangerous, but it's fantastic in its own way.

Because it's closer.

It's more intimate.

It's a connection I didn't expect but can't deny.

"I love the way you feel so deep in me," she murmurs.

Deep in her. That's precisely how it is with Mackenzie. Like I'm getting lost in her, and I don't want to be found. Gone is the rushing, the fevered race to the end. Instead, we're sliding and moaning with slow, indulgent delight.

Soon, our sounds mingle, layering on top of each other. Pants, and groans, and sighs.

So good.
Keep doing that.
It feels incredible.
You. God, you.

Pleasure ricochets down my spine, electrifying me.

Mackenzie arches up, her hands slinking into my hair, her fingers tousling through it as she desperately whispers, "You're making me come again."

Hottest words ever.

When she cries out, tipping over, I'm falling off the cliff too.

My brain goes haywire. My mind is a blur. I'm so far gone in her. I say her name, and I let go, joining her on the other side.

When I open my eyes, a million thoughts form on my tongue, but I don't say a word. Our eyes say everything when our gazes lock.

She has to be able to tell from how I look at her.

From the way I kiss her cheek, the corner of her lips, her eyelids.

From how I breathe her name reverently. "Mackenzie."

She has to know I'm falling in love with her.

CHAPTER 21

Campbell

Campbell: Just so you know I'm still thinking of that. Of you.

Mackenzie: Me too. It's on a nonstop loop in my head.

Campbell: We were pretty amazing the first time but that was . . .

Mackenzie: Dope?

Campbell: Is that what we call it now? When something is amazing?

Mackenzie: Dope or sick. Both of which feel incredibly wrong as a way to describe amazing sex, even though everyone says you can't say epic anymore.

Campbell: Felt epic to me. :)

Mackenzie: Me too.

Campbell: Can we agree that we're totally okay using epic to describe the kind of sex we had?

Mackenzie: It was beyond epic. How's that?

Campbell: *thumps chest in epic victory*

Mackenzie: But on a more serious note, I feel like I should feel bad if we keep having epic sex.

Campbell: Do you feel bad? I don't want you to feel bad about anything.

Mackenzie: The weird thing—I don't. I thought I would. I've tried to resist you. Maybe I haven't tried hard enough, but I have tried.

Campbell: Do you want points for effort? Happy to give them to you. :)

Mackenzie: No, that's not what I'm saying. I think what I'm saying is this—I expected to feel more guilt since my head has been telling me to resist you. But I don't feel that way.

Campbell: How do you feel?

Mackenzie: It might be the orgasm talking, but I feel pretty damn good.

Campbell: I'd like to make sure the orgasm keeps talking, then.

Mackenzie: The O has spoken.

* * *

We're bad again, like a couple of junkies. We sneak in a midday session on Tuesday and another on Wednesday after lunch. Damn, it's fantastic messing around with a woman who keeps her own schedule. It makes it a piece of cake to slip away for some afternoon delight at her place.

Each time I'm tempted to say something, to give voice to the words that have been teasing at my mind —*I'm falling for you*. But Mackenzie established the rules of engagement. Since she has more at stake than I do, I need to respect her guidelines.

But it sure as hell feels like we're this close to breaking the new rules when I sneak over to her place for a Thursday lunch that feels like a date. I take her hard and fast as she bends over the bed. I fuck her the way she likes it, rough and fast, bringing her two orgasms before I let myself finish.

I'm a generous fucker, pun intended.

I'm still panting, still sweating as I say, "That was . . ."

"Incredible?" she supplies.

"It was incredible."

We flop down on the bed together, and she turns to loop her arms around my neck, threading her fingers through my hair. "So are you."

My heart rolls over in my chest, and I want to say it now. *I'm falling so hard for you.*

I smother the thought with a hot, wet kiss, followed by a fantastic chicken and cheddar panini she makes me for lunch.

* * *

That night, we text each other. She confesses she's never seen *My Crazy Ex-Girlfriend*. It's a musical, a comedy, and a spoof, so I tell her it's a crime she's never watched it.

Since our kids are asleep, we tune in to an episode together on the phone.

"Damn, you're right. That's a fine, fine show," she says when the episode ends. "Also, watching TV together on the phone—are we dorks?"

"Kind of?"

She laughs. "I think it might be more than kind of. It has to be full dorkitude."

"We are epic dorks."

But I like it that way, and I like her in every way. "See you at Kyle's lesson tomorrow. I'll pretend I'm not thinking of you naked."

* * *

For the first time, I struggle to look her son in the eye when I go to her home the next day. But that's not because I'm thinking of his mom naked. It's because of how I feel for his mom.

As I work with Kyle, a stark, new awareness dawns on me. I thought Mackenzie was the one who had more at stake, but now I see what's at stake for me.

I care deeply for her son. I like working with him. I want to see him succeed. That's why I don't want to be the music teacher who screws students' moms. I don't want to have that rep, with Kyle or with anyone.

I want to be better than that. I want to set an example, not just for my daughter, but for all the kids I work with.

Trouble is, I don't know how to do that if I'm sneaking around and keeping my true feelings a dirty little secret.

CHAPTER 22

Mackenzie

Roxy palms an extra-wide zucchini at the farmers market that weekend. "So, the resistance is working out well for you?"

I stick my tongue out at her.

"Wait, wasn't that what he did to you?" Roxy asks, deadpan.

I stare at her. "He did, and it was spectacular," I say as the memory of the spontaneous sex with Campbell from the other night sizzles me from head to toe. And the bend-over-the-bed sex the next day. And the get-on-all-fours-now kind we had the day after. And the texts he sends me.

The *thinking of you as I'm falling asleep* notes. The *still thinking of you as I wake up* ones.

Tingles zip down my chest. They're so dangerous, but so delicious. He makes me shiver all over, inside and out. I don't know what to do with all these new emotions—they feel so damn good I can't find it in me to turn them down.

"Lucky bitch." Roxy flicks her red hair off her shoulder then stares studiously at the veggie in her hand.

"It was definitely 'lucky bitch' sex with him. But then, sex with Campbell has been of the 'lucky bitch' variety since the start."

"Not jealous. Not jealous at all," she mutters as she sets down the long green veggie. She lowers her voice so the bearded guy running the stall can't hear. "I always think I'll like zucchini by itself. But it's a trick. Zucchini fools you with that shape. It's like a super-hot guy who's really dull inside."

"Like the guy from the subway?"

She rolls her eyes. "So dull. He was eggplant-level dull."

"Whoa. That's saying a lot for you to compare him to an eggplant."

"Exactly. I'm telling you, it's getting to the point where I'm going to call a cease-fire on all dating. I'm going to march straight to the nearest sperm bank and put my money down on a tall Harvard man who loves puppies."

My eyes nearly pop out. "Are you serious?"

She nods vigorously. "Must love dogs is critical, don't you think?"

"No. I mean are you serious about the sperm bank thing?"

She shrugs. "Maybe. Someday. I like kids. I like men too. The problem is, finding a straight, interesting, loyal guy who doesn't live at home is nearly as challenging as making a zucchini taste good raw."

She makes a fair point. "The problem with zucchini and eggplant is you have to dress them up too much."

"Exactly," Roxy seconds. "With zucchini, it's only tolerable if it's hidden among other veggies. With eggplant, it has to trick everybody with sauce slathered all over it. It has no actual taste on its own."

"Thank God for zucchini bread, then."

"Amen. That's the only form I actually like zucchini in, and then it better practically be zucchini cake."

We wander to the next stall. It's lush with mushrooms of all shapes and varieties, shiitake and cremini and a beautiful basket of chanterelles too. "But mushrooms are so yummy."

"Does that mean your guy," she says, strolling

past the portobellos, "is like a delicious dish of sautéed mushrooms?"

I crinkle my nose. "It's weird to think about non-phallic vegetables to describe a man. But mushrooms are pretty freaking tasty." I count off on my fingers. "So is roasted broccoli with parmesan cheese, so are green beans with sesame seeds and garlic, and so are fried artichoke hearts."

She stares at me with hunger in her eyes. "Thanks. Now my mouth is watering, and I'm going to kidnap you so you can make all those dishes for me, because they sound incredible."

"They do sound good," I say as I select some mushrooms, since I'll start with that for dinner. But I definitely need to make fried artichoke hearts too. As I choose the mushrooms, an idea pops into my head. "I bet Campbell's daughter would like making fried artichoke hearts with me. She gets a kick out of learning to cook new savory dishes, since she focuses more on sweets. She loves figuring things out in the kitchen and trying new recipes."

Roxy freezes while riffling through the morels. "Oh my God, you're falling for his kid too."

"What?" I scoff as I meet her wide eyes.

She points at me as if I'm the guilty suspect she's ID'd in a police lineup. "You're totally into his kid."

I flub my lips. "Yeah, she's cool. But I'm not falling for her—or him, for that matter."

Roxy arches a most skeptical brow as I buy the mushrooms, including the morels for her.

"It's only sex," I whisper as we leave the mushroom stall.

"But you do like having sex with him."

"Duh. He gives me multiples, and he's a rock star in bed."

"And out of it," she says under her breath.

"He's also a really interesting guy, and we have great conversations, and his daughter is fun, but that's all there is. I'm not falling for him. I'm not falling for either one of them."

"I guess it's a good thing you're not dating him. I mean, you wouldn't want to give it a go with him or anything like that. Perish the thought."

"Roxy, dating him isn't even possible." We wander down the row, and I scan over the green beans and sugar snap peas, searching for artichokes. "Kyle is doing so well with Campbell as a teacher. He has a concert coming up at the end of the week that he's so excited about. And besides, even if I did pursue something, what are the chances it would work out?"

Roxy raises a finger. "Now we're getting somewhere. That's your concern, isn't it? Not whether you're falling for him."

I sigh heavily. "I can't think about falling for him. I don't have a great track record with men. Don't forget I'm the girl who got knocked up her last year of college, then graduated while sporting a baby bump."

"And you haven't even tried to date seriously since then."

"I've dated. There have been a few guys." I rattle off a couple names of men I've gone on more than a few dates with over the last thirteen years. Hmm. That's a short list.

"And none of those guys have turned into anything serious. It's not as if you brought any of them over to meet Kyle." She drapes an arm around me. "I get that he's your number one priority. I'm not suggesting he should be anything but that." She squeezes my shoulder and takes a beat. "But do you think maybe you've held back when it comes to dating because you're afraid of your own supposed track record?"

"Hello? Considering my accidental pregnancy at age twenty also derailed my career plans, it seems a reasonable concern."

"This is my point exactly." She levels me with her gaze over a table of arugula. "You haven't forgiven yourself for getting pregnant so young, and you don't give yourself a chance to be anything but supermom. It's like if you're less than supermom, you'll slip up again, so you avoid taking chances."

"But . . ." I have nothing to say. She's right. I don't

take big chances when it comes to men. I make safe choices or no choices.

Though lately, I've been making secret choices, and those aren't the best ones either.

Which also proves my point—I'm a screwup when it comes to romance.

Roxy's eyes light up. She grabs a bundle of asparagus and heads to the vendor to pay for it. But as she sets it in her canvas bag, her words keep nagging at me.

We leave the stall, and I ask her a question. I'm not sure I want her answer, but I probably need to hear it. "Do you really think I stress about my *checkered past*?"

"I do. I really think you do. I think you need to let it go. It's not like you've done something terrible. You turned something unplanned into something completely beautiful. You've carved out a wonderful life for you, your son, and your son's father, and you have this cool, random modern family. Your kid is doing great. You're a talented graphic designer, and you've built a business of your own that's way better than any corporate gig you'd have had if you'd taken the job with that ad agency."

Not taking the job after college was a risk, but it turned into a fantastic reward over time, given how my solo business has grown by leaps and bounds. "That's true."

"Plus, you're a terrific friend and a fantastic cook. You've turned everything into, well, into a delish slice of zucchini bread."

"I do like a good zucchini bread."

"Come here." She grabs my arm and pulls me to a vendor selling sweets. She buys a few items then hands me a small slice of bread. "Try this."

I bite into it, and my taste buds sing hallelujah. "It's tasty."

"See? Zucchini bread can sometimes taste exactly like cake."

But even as I chew, I'm not sure zucchini cake is what I want. You can't have something this tasty every day.

* * *

When Friday night rolls around, I help Kyle adjust his tie, and we walk ten blocks to the community center for the fall concert. Parents are hustling and bustling inside, since most of the performers are kids from various schools in the city.

I find Jamison quickly. He's in the auditorium, smiling and looking handsome. He gives Kyle a hug and then a high five. "Go get 'em, tiger," he says.

As Kyle heads backstage, I'm reminded he's reason enough not to go further with Campbell. I don't want to ruin a good thing, and what Kyle and Campbell have is a very good thing.

Jamison and I take our seats. We catch up briefly on his production of *Chicago*, and he asks how work is going with a new agency client of mine. Swimmingly, is the answer for both of us.

Just like Roxy said.

There goes one of her check marks—I definitely have a kick-ass job. It's a job I didn't expect to have thirteen years ago. I never set out to have this career, but I do love it madly.

I love my crazy friendship with my son's father too, even though that's certainly something I never thought my college bestie and I would team up on—raising a kid. Funny how so many unexpected moments turned into welcome opportunities.

But even so, that doesn't mean every unexpected moment will or can.

Be content with what you have.

After a few minutes, I feel a hand on my shoulder. Warmth zips through me, and for a brief moment, I'm terrified the hand will belong to somebody I shouldn't feel a spark from whatsoever. But when I look up, green eyes and a gorgeous jawline greet me.

A glow seems to spread in my chest, and tingles race down my arms—a new cocktail of twin sensations. Desire and happiness fill me as I look at the handsome man standing next to me.

"I didn't realize you were coming," I say.

Campbell is with his daughter, who waves at me. "Hi, Mackenzie. I can't wait to hear Kyle perform."

"And I wouldn't miss this for anything," Campbell says, and my heart goes swoon.

Silly organ. Swooning is for kids.

They sit next to us, and soon Sam and Jamison are talking about *Hamilton*. "I've seen it five times, and I swear it gets better every single time," Sam tells Jamison.

His jaw comes unhinged. "Girl, I cannot even with you. I've only seen it three times. It's literally the best show in the universe."

"I know! I'm going again in a few weeks."

I snap my gaze to her. "You're going a sixth time? I've only seen it once, and I basically had to sell my soul to the devil to get the ticket."

Jamison smiles wickedly and taps his chest. "I'm the devil she speaks of. And it wasn't that hard. I just called my friends on the show."

"Oh, it was hard," I correct. "You had to call ten times."

He huffs. "It wasn't that many times."

I turn to Sam. "So what's *your* secret?"

She smiles impishly and tips her forehead to her dad.

Campbell grins, a gorgeous, lopsided smile that dares to make my heart kick over. But I remind my heart to settle down. "What's your secret? Did you pull the Heartbreaker card?"

He nods then blows on his fingers. "It comes in handy from time to time. Not to mention the 'I used to be in *Les Mis*' card."

Jamison jumps in. "You need to kick it up a notch. You should totally play Jean Valjean next. That would be mind-blowing to see you as the lead in a revival."

"Yeah, Dad. That would be cool."

Campbell laughs, shaking his head. "I don't know if I can pull off Valjean. He has quite the range."

Jamison holds up a finger. "Listen, if you ever want to play Jean Valjean, you better come to me, and we will talk about putting together a production. I will pull whatever strings I can possibly reach to produce a revival with you as 24601."

I turn toward Campbell, lowering my voice. "If you played the lead, I'd see you three times. Maybe even five."

"Is that so? You'd be a *Les Mis* fangirl?" he asks playfully.

I drop to a full whisper. "I would throw my panties on stage if you were Valjean."

"That's quite an incentive. I'll consider it more seriously now."

"You do that."

Silence descends over the auditorium as the curtain rises. All eyes turn to the stage as the concert begins. A classical guitarist plays a song, and he's followed by a brass band. A trio of girls comes on next, singing a cappella. These kids are all good, and it's a delight to watch the different groups of middle and high schoolers.

At the end, the string quartet comes on stage—two violins, a cello, and a viola. They're the closing act of the concert. These four kids are the ones who are most serious about music, and it shows.

They shift from Brahms to Beethoven to Arcade Fire to Jay-Z, and goosebumps erupt on my skin with every piece. It's beautiful and uplifting at the same time as they play a mix of classical and rock.

When it ends, Jamison and I are on our feet, clapping and cheering. "Bravo!"

The musicians bow to another round of thunderous applause. I turn to Campbell and throw my arms around him. "You're amazing. You did this."

He tugs me close and shakes his head. "No, he did this. I told you, the kid's talented."

I smile in his arms, savoring the strength of his embrace and the manly smell of him as I catch a faint whiff of his neck. I let the hug last a little longer than it should, because it feels so good right now. So right too. Like this is exactly how life should work out—him attending a concert my kid's performing in.

But that's what terrifies me too.

I don't know how this feeling could possibly last long enough to make the risk worthwhile.

Because as I look to the stage and Kyle's smiling face, the pride in his eyes, I don't want to risk a thing that might hurt him.

* * *

Later that night, Kyle is still on a high from the show. He's practically bouncing off the walls in our apartment, recapping the performance. Which is precisely how I can tell he's like a dog who needs to be run.

"You need to burn off some of that energy. Why don't we go wild tonight?"

He stops pacing across the living room. "Let me guess, Mom. That means milkshakes and fries?"

I nod excitedly as I clean the kitchen counter—my way of blowing off excess energy. "What else could I possibly mean?"

"I can't think of a thing I'd rather do than get a milkshake and fries at nine thirty on a Friday."

"We know how to party." I'm grabbing my coat, scarf, and hat when my mind slings back in time. "Want to try a new place? Campbell recommended a great diner called Willy G's in Murray Hill. He said it's the best."

Kyle flashes a toothy grin. "Sounds cool. Let's go." He swipes his phone from the coffee table and says, "Hold on. I need to text a friend."

"You can bring someone if you want," I offer as I tug the light-blue knit cap down on my head. November has ushered in chilly nights.

"It's cool, Mom. I don't need to bring anyone. I just need to text someone."

Twenty minutes later, after a hearty subway review of our all-time favorite scenes from Harry Potter—riding the dragon out of Gringotts ranks near the top—we arrive at the bustling diner in Campbell's hood.

Even though I'm not thinking of him at all.

Just like I wasn't checking him out at The Grouchy Owl.

As I grab the handle of the door, savoring the rush of warm air that brings with it the smell of diner food, grease, and burgers, I toss out a question to my son. "On a scale of one to ten, how awesome are diners?"

Kyle rolls his eyes. "Mom, they don't make scales that high."

"That is the perfect answer."

Diners are one of my favorite aspects of New York. I've been to diners around the country, and I've never encountered one that can compare to those we have in Manhattan. Call me a New York diner snob. I'll own it. New York diners are the best in the world, and they're one of the reasons I've chosen to cobble together a life for the two of us in the city. Diners, Broadway shows, art, museums, friends, family, sports, and entertainment. I love everything the city has to offer.

Including milkshakes and fries.

Once we're inside, a curly-haired woman in a mint-green waitress uniform tells us to grab a booth. We choose a big one near the back, slide into the orange vinyl seats, and peruse the menu. I shake my head as I stare at the plethora of offerings. "Why am I even looking? I know what I'm getting."

"Milkshake and fries."

The words come out in a deep rumble, and they're not from my son.

I look up from the menu to see the man I'm crazy for.

CHAPTER 23

Campbell

"Hey?"

She says it like a question, her expression one of complete surprise. Her gaze connects with mine then with Sam's next to me.

"Fancy meeting you here," I say, but I'm surprised too. Sam was the one who spotted the two of them when we strolled into the diner a minute ago.

"You mentioned this place once," Mackenzie says quickly. A faint blush spreads over her cheeks, reminding me she knows exactly when that *once* was —the first time she took me home. She waves her hand as if she has to dismiss that thought, lest it turn her cheeks to two bright spots of apple red. "I've wanted to try it ever since."

I smile, hoping it conveys my meaning—*I remember that night. I remember the time I mentioned this place to you in bed.* "It's the best. Sam loves it as well. It was her idea to come here tonight."

Mackenzie creases her brow. "Oh. It was?"

She looks to Kyle, whose face is buried in the menu, studying it like his life depends on memorizing the plastic-covered pages.

I catch the faint hint of a smirk on his lips though, and when I glance at Sam, she's wearing a matching smirk.

I have a hunch who might've come up with the idea to go to this place tonight—these two kids. I'm not sure how the plan originated, or if the two of them simply played messenger, but I'm willing to bet this serendipitous meeting is less happenstance than I'd thought it was. They might have been puppeteers.

"Want to join us?" Mackenzie asks.

"We'd love to," Sam answers quickly, her speed further confirming my suspicions.

We order, and as we wait for our food, the kids dive into a discussion of *Fortnite*, funny memes, and music they like.

Mackenzie and I do the same, only we launch into a postmortem on the latest episode of *The Discovery Prism Show*.

"Did you see that one about some of the quirky places in the mid-Atlantic?" she asks.

"Like the cavern with the great stalactite organ?"

Her face lights up. "Yes. Isn't that the coolest thing in the world? I really want to go see that at some point."

Deep underground in the caves of Virginia is a church organ that looks normal at first. Turns out that the pipes are made of the stalactites, and when the keys are struck the entire cave becomes a musical instrument. The organ in the cave plays classics like "America the Beautiful," "Moonlight Sonata," and "Silent Night."

"I'd love to visit that too. And the Victrola Museum. It's not that far away since it's in Delaware. Did you see the episode with the Victrola Museum?"

She shakes her head. "Missed that one."

If she hasn't seen it, I take a gamble she might not know one of the quirkiest trivia bits about that museum. "That's where the phrase 'put a sock in it' comes from."

A flash of curiosity crosses her eyes. "It does?"

"That's what people used to suggest to neighbors with Victrola horns, so they'd lower the volume when they played them too loudly. Or did you know that already? It's probably one of your trivia answers that's super easy."

She laughs, shaking her head. "You can ask me

the Victrola dog's name—Nipper, his breed—mixed terrier, and whether Victor was the largest maker of musical instruments for many years—yes. But if you'd asked where the famous phrase 'put a sock in it' originated from, I just learned that about two seconds ago."

I pump a fist. "Damn. I've accomplished the impossible."

"Well done."

"Have you seen the episode on Sydney?"

"No, but I keep meaning to check it out."

"Me too..."

I smile, and she smiles back like we have a little secret, and like she wants me to ask her on another clandestine date. The funny thing is our Netflix phone dates have been some of the best I've ever had, and I know if we do it again, it will be another great date.

The trouble is I want more than a phone date.

More than a secret meetup.

I want it all.

And I don't want to wait much longer.

The waitress arrives with the fries and shakes. We thank her, and Sam says, "Let's toast." She raises her silver tumbler.

"What are we toasting to?" I ask.

"To slammin' plans."

I give her a look. "Slammin' plans? What exactly are these slammin' plans?"

She pats my hand. "Don't you worry your pretty little head about it, Daddy-o." She casts her gaze to Kyle.

He's holding in a laugh as he sucks the shake through a straw. "We can't tell you just yet."

Mackenzie's lips part in question. "We? The two of you have these slammin' plans?"

"We have secrets," Samantha confirms confidently.

I raise my glass. "Then we shall toast to secrets we will absolutely get to the bottom of."

I mean it to be funny, but instantly a pang of guilt traverses my chest. Because we're the ones keeping secrets from our kids.

Neither Mackenzie nor I have voiced it, but I'm pretty damn sure our hearts are on the same page. I know from how she smiles at me. From the glorious hug she wrapped me in earlier. I know from the way she wants to watch a show together again on the phone, and I know from how she's kissed me, how she's talked to me, and how she's come as close as she'll let herself to sharing her heart.

She's told me she thinks I am incredible.

And I think the same damn thing about her.

When her eyes lock with mine as she brings her

cup to her lips, I'm certain this is something real. She knows how I feel.

The same.

She feels the same way I do.

That's why this guilt cuts deeper. Stabs harder.

My guilt isn't about sex.

Sex is private. Sex is personal, and my guilt doesn't stem from the fact that my daughter doesn't know who I'm sleeping with. She doesn't need to know that.

But she sure as hell should know who I care for. Who I want to date. Who I want to make a part of her life.

After we work our way through fries and milkshakes, Samantha gestures to Kyle. "You know they have a jukebox here?"

"Let's go check it out," Kyle says.

They scoot out of the booth, and as soon as they're down the row, I slide a hand under the table. I grab Mackenzie's, and she threads her fingers through mine. "Hey, Sunshine," I say in a low voice.

Her eyelids flutter. "Hey, sexy," she says.

"You look beautiful."

She glances down at her outfit. "In my jeans and sweater?"

"Yes, in your jeans and sweater, you look absolutely stunning."

"I have a hat too. Want to see it?" She grabs a hat

from the seat next to her and models it, looking like a snow bunny, like Claudia Schiffer at the end of *Love Actually*.

My heart does somersaults, and my voice is rough as I say, "You look stunning in a hat. You look stunning in everything. I want it to snow so you can go outside and I can kiss you in the snow."

She links her hand tighter with mine. "I want that."

Emboldened by her response, I blurt out the wish in my heart. "Go out with me."

She blinks. "What?"

"On a date."

"Like we were going to have?"

I glance at the corner of the diner. Sam and Kyle are chatting animatedly at the jukebox. "Yes. I want you to go out with me. For real. In the open."

"Like, we'd tell the kids?"

I nod, feeling a surge of excitement. Feeling *right*. "Yes."

Worry flashes across her features as she tips her chin toward the children. "Do you think they know?"

"I don't know. Maybe we're terrible at hiding our feelings."

Her eyes meet mine. They're wide and full of emotion. "We might be, because I feel like they're trying to *Parent Trap* us."

I raise a brow. "Parent trap?"

"It's a film. Lindsay Lohan played identical twins in her film debut, an update of a 1961 Disney movie," she says, then waves her hand. "The details don't matter. The point is the kids tried to get their parents back together."

"So you think they know?"

"What is it they know, Campbell?" she asks softly, her tone inviting me to tell her more.

I squeeze her hand under the table. "I think they know I'm crazy for you." My skin warms, and my heart thumps harder, waiting for a response from her.

It comes quickly as a smile stretches across her face. "I bet they know I'm crazy for you too."

Now I'm grinning like a happy fool. "Smart kids."

"So smart," she says, and somehow her smile is impossibly bigger and even more beautiful.

"I think they engineered this whole 'milkshake and fries' thing tonight."

"That would be okay with me. That they're okay with us," she says with relief in her voice, like their approval is all she'd ever want.

Shoes squeak on linoleum, and we drop hands like they're on fire.

A split second later, Samantha and Kyle appear at the booth, wide grins on their faces.

"We have something super exciting we want to tell you," Samantha says, bouncing in her Adidas.

"It's dope," Kyle seconds.

Mackenzie's grin is bigger than both of theirs. "Tell us. We're ready."

"We are so ready," I add, excitement bubbling over in me. The possibility that they might want us to be together is thrilling.

Samantha spreads her hands. "Picture this: a rock music string quartet with a certain lead singer."

Kyle points wildly at me. "And we want you to be our teacher. Would you be willing to do that? Not just do lessons for me, but be like a coach for the whole string quartet? Samantha is going to be our singer, and we could play at more places in Manhattan and be like a cool, new modern rock band."

My jaw nearly comes unhinged.

This isn't a parent trap whatsoever.

This isn't kids trying to engineer two adults into dating.

This was two adults foolishly thinking their desire to date matched the interests of their teenagers.

What fools we were.

What these kids want isn't for us to be a happy, blended Brady family. They want their lives to roll on normally. That's all they're thinking. That's all they *should* be thinking.

I look at Mackenzie, and when our eyes meet, all

her emotions are clear—sadness and resignation. We feel the same for each other, so we feel the same heavy disappointment now too. She swallows and nods, as if it's painful. I understand those twin gestures completely—we need to do what's best for them.

Be friends. Be parents. Be supportive of their dreams.

Not be lovers who might not work out. Who might split up. Who might put their needs ahead of the kids'.

"I'd be happy to teach your new quartet. Or is it really a quintet?" I ask, wryly.

"Yes!" Sam thrusts an arm in the air in victory. "We're a quintet."

They take off and return to the jukebox.

I sigh, dragging a hand through my hair as I gaze at Mackenzie. "I guess we wanted to believe they wanted the same thing we do."

Her voice is heavy. "Foolish hope?"

I nod, with a small self-deprecating smile—a fool's smile. "It was. Wasn't it?"

She sighs. "They're not hoping we'll be together, Campbell."

"Yeah, I know. They're kids. They just want to be kids. They want to learn and have fun and explore the world."

"I want that for them."

And that's part of why I've fallen for her—because she wants that as badly as I do. "Me too."

She takes a beat. "I'm still crazy for you, but maybe that means we should table this—us."

I swallow harshly. "I'm still crazy for you too. But maybe we should keep things the way they are."

Her shoulders drop. "If they're going to be playing together, it'll be for the best for them, don't you think?"

I do. That's the kicker. I do think it's best if we keep putting them first. That's what I vowed to do more than a decade ago. That's what I've always done. Mackenzie isn't some random woman who's unconnected to my family. If that were the case, I could date her no problem. But she's wrapped up in my life now, and I'm tangled up in hers.

That's a recipe for messy complications down the line.

I nod. "Keep everything stable and safe—that's what we want."

"Yes."

Those words echo—*stable and safe*. That's what matters most to both of us. That's why, for the rest of the evening, we don't hold hands anymore.

* * *

I get into bed after midnight, running my thumb over the phone. I want to text her. To say something. To say anything. But if we keep texting, we'll keep calling, we'll keep watching, and we'll keep screwing.

We can't do those things anymore.

Campbell: I guess we should stop texting, since we're going to be good once and for all now.

Mackenzie: You're probably right. We'll go back to being . . . mom and teacher?

It pains me to say yes, but that's what I need to say. I rip off the Band-Aid.

Campbell: Yes.

Mackenzie: Okay.

Campbell: Bye.

Mackenzie: Bye.

I fear we could do this all night long, and somebody has to put a stop to it, so I don't reply.

CHAPTER 24

Mackenzie

Everything hurts.

My heart hurts.

My head hurts.

Right now though? My legs are crying out for mercy.

My thighs are burning up something fierce, courtesy of the spin fundraiser Jamison and I are cycling in to raise money for leukemia on a Saturday morning.

As always, he's festive and cheery as he power-rides in place. "The string quartet is so cute. Aren't they adorable?"

"Yeah."

He cycles, his chest high, his chin up, like he has all the energy in the world. "They sound so good. I went to their practice the other night. They were brilliant in concert, and they're already ten thousand times better with Sam singing vocals."

That's an exaggeration. They're maybe 3 percent better, though that's still impressive. They do have a terrific coach-slash-instructor who gives his all to the kids.

"Campbell is kicking butt at teaching them," Jamison adds.

"Yeah." My voice is as flat as my heart.

"And Sam! What a set of pipes she has. No surprise there though. I guess it's in her genes."

"Yup."

Jamison snaps his gaze to me. "Did someone poison your pie?"

I wince, thinking of the arsenic joke Campbell made the night we met at The Grouchy Owl. I shake my head. "No. This is just hard."

He stares sharply at me, seeing through my bald-faced lie as he pedals like the wind is beneath his sails. "You've been training for months. You can do this in your sleep."

I laugh harshly. "I can't cycle in my sleep. It's kind of hard."

But the fact is I can do better, so I focus, cycling harder, though I wish this were easier. Not the riding, but the ending things.

The cold-turkey Campbell sandwich I've been eating tastes terrible.

It's like a dish of misery, chased by a glass of bitter sadness.

We haven't had any contact except at lessons, and I've stayed out of the way during those.

We haven't texted. We haven't called each other. We haven't watched shows together, and we haven't accidentally or purposefully landed naked in each other's beds. I also haven't gone to his home to make videos or share recipes with his daughter.

That makes my heart hurt even more. I like Samantha, and I miss her too.

I've done my best to throw myself into work, tossing all my energy and focus into a new design project. But when I work on a sunburst effect, I think of his damn tattoo.

And that makes it harder to concentrate.

He's everywhere. Everything reminds me of him.

Life is so unfair. Who decided breakups had to hurt worse than stepping on Legos?

When the cycling event ends, Jamison thrusts both arms in the air, hops off his bike, and congratulates me on crushing it.

I leave the room on jelly legs and want to smack

myself for even thinking of that adjective. That's what Campbell did to me the first night we were together—he gave me four orgasms and reduced me to jelly.

But it's not the Os I miss madly. It's the man.

In the lobby of the gym, Jamison and I grab some water.

"You know why I think your pie is poisoned?"

I take the bait. "Why?"

"The guy. It's about a guy."

"Oh, is it?"

He smirks. "It's the music teacher. You've had a crush on him forever. And for what it's worth, I think you should just tell him."

I scoff, like he didn't just nail it, and I toss my hair. "Please."

Jamison rolls his eyes. "Don't deny it, Mackenzie. It's so obvious you might as well have it tattooed on your forehead."

"Is that so?"

"Give me some credit. I could tell at the concert. The way you looked at him. The way he looked at you. That's how you look at Idris Elba. That's the way we all look at Thor."

I laugh. "You're ridiculous."

"Everyone loves Thor."

"True," I acknowledge, because that's as true as the law of gravity.

"And look, if Thor wanted you the same way the rest of the world wanted him, I'd tell you to go for it. You should just go for it with Campbell."

"It's not that simple," I say a little mournfully.

He shrugs. "Why not? Some things *are* simple."

"He's Kyle's teacher."

Jamison clutches his cheeks. "Oh my God. You're right. That means you should never ever touch him."

"I'm serious."

He shrugs it off. "There's always something. What's the worst that's going to happen? You go out with him, he turns out to be a big jackwad, you break up with him, we find a new teacher?" He snaps his fingers. "Done. If he breaks your heart, I will bake him into a meat pie like Sweeney Todd, and I'll find a new teacher who's better than *42nd Street*."

I laugh lightly. "I love you and your revenge plans. But in reality, Kyle adores him. Kyle is thriving with him."

Jamison parks his hands on his hips. "Kids are resilient, Mackenzie. Kyle is doing great because we've raised a great kid. Don't sacrifice your own happiness over this."

"But how do I know if I can be happy with Campbell? How do I know if it's worth the Sweeney Todd exit plan if it gets to that point?"

What if he breaks my heart? The thought terrifies

me, since my heart feels like it already belongs to him, and that gives him power over its fate.

But what if he... doesn't break it?

"You don't. You take your chance anyway," he says.

I toss up my hands. I'm tired of talking in circles. "Actually, screw it. You might as well know the truth. We had a thing going for a bit. And it was wonderful, because he's wonderful. But we decided to end things because of the kids."

A gleam of triumph flashes in Jamison's blue eyes. "I knew it! I knew there was something between the two of you. And you have to tell me everything now."

He grabs my wrist, steals me away to a coffee shop, and plies me with lattes until I confess. For the record, a vanilla latte is all I need as truth serum.

Jamison bangs his fists on the table, hoots and hollers as I share the basic details. "You two are so perfect together, it's disgusting, but in a beautiful kind of way," he says.

I laugh. "Well, thanks. Glad you find us gross."

"Gross and lovely and perfect. I approve. And now you can't back down. You absolutely have to go for this. This is so much more than I thought it was." He reaches across the table and squeezes my hand. "Kyle would totally understand."

"Do you really think so?"

As Jamison nods, a kernel of hope rises in me, a bubble of possibility. "Absolutely," he says then adds, "You know, you could actually talk to Kyle and discuss it with him. See how he feels."

I shiver. The thought is vaguely terrifying. "I don't want to mess things up if he's happy."

"You don't give yourself enough credit for how good you are at pulling stuff off."

I shoot him a skeptical look. "You think I'm good at that?"

"I absolutely do. And you are a primo juggler." He mimes juggling. "You're not just good at pulling stuff off. You're great at it. Look at you and me, you and Kyle, you and graphic design. You know how to figure things out. Now, stop being so scared and go for it."

Go for it.

Should I?

Have I been wrong all along about my track record?

I've always thought it was flawed. But maybe I've been looking at my life through the wrong prism. Perhaps I have figured out how to make the best of the unexpected. The unexpected pregnancy, the unexpected career change—I turned those curveballs into home runs.

Campbell has been unexpected too, I suppose. I never thought I'd fall for a one-night stand, and I never thought he'd turn out to be the guy I'm in love with.

Because that's what it is with Campbell.

That's why I'm so damn sad.

I love that guy.

I want him as mine.

CHAPTER 25

Campbell

"How does that sound for a set list?"

My sneakers hit the dirt in Central Park as I run up a hill with JJ.

"Great," I answer, though I have no clue what songs he's rattled off. I've been thinking of Mackenzie most of the run. Wondering what she's up to. Curious how her week has been.

"Excellent. We'll sing 'London Bridge is Falling Down,' then."

I snap my gaze to my bandmate. "What?"

JJ laughs heartily. "Dude, you have no clue what I've been talking about."

"Sure I do." I try to cover up my lack of attention.

"You've been talking about how great it is that the Righteous Surfboards have turned into something, how we have a following, and then we were reviewing songs for our next gig at The Grouchy Owl."

He rolls his eyes as we crest the hill. "I said that five minutes ago."

Busted.

"Sorry. I was focused on running."

He scoffs. "I don't think you're focused on running. You've been distracted all week long."

"I have?"

The fall air is brisk, and the wind whips past us. "You've been elsewhere, man. You've barely focused on anything I said about the band. Do you still want to do this?"

I bristle at the suggestion that I'm not all in. "Of course."

He smacks my arm. "Then maybe you need to figure out why you haven't been able to stay focused. It's okay if you have shit on your mind. I respect that. Just be honest with me about it. Do you need a break?"

I need a break from my own thoughts.

I need a break from the fact that I fucking miss Mackenzie like it's a religion.

But, most of all, what I need a break from is the break.

Not talking to her daily is brutal. Sam and the string quartet kids are having a blast, but I'd be having an even better time if the four of us could hang out together again—Mackenzie, Sam, Kyle, and me.

That's the craziest thing. I don't just miss the woman. I miss hanging out with her and her kid. I miss her spending time with my kid, and I long for the moments when the four of us were together.

That's what I want back. All of it. I want Mackenzie, and I want the four of us.

I want it all.

Somehow.

"No. I don't need a break," I tell JJ as we hit a flat section of the path, and I give him my focus like he deserves.

When we're done, I'm tempted to call Mackenzie. To try to figure out how to pull this off. But I'm not ready yet. I need to devise a game plan. I need to talk to someone else.

But that someone's not home when I return from my run. She's out at soccer practice, and maybe that's for the best since I'm not sure yet what to say.

I choose plan B when Miller texts and asks me to meet him for lunch.

Miller is always happy. Maybe it'll rub off on me.

CHAPTER 26

Mackenzie

"—came from what instrument?"

My mind barely registers the words from the hostess at the new pub we've been trying out for Saturday afternoon trivia. All I can think about are Jamison's words earlier today. His advice. His encouragement. That's the only thing on my mind.

Roxy snaps her fingers in front of me. "Earth to Mackenzie."

I blink and find Roxy staring at me, her eyes like a bullfrog's.

"What?"

"The question," she says urgently. "How do you

not know it? I thought this would for sure be something you knew."

My shoulders sag. "I totally missed the question. I'm sorry. I was drifting off."

"The saying 'put a sock in it' came from what—"

A buzzer sounds from the hostess's phone. "Time's up."

I groan as I stare at the blank answer line for that question. "It's Victrola. I suck."

Roxy's expression softens, and she pats my hand. "You've been like this all day. Did you have a lobotomy, or did the aliens take over last night?"

I laugh sadly. "I'm just thinking."

"I can tell. I can literally see the cogs turning in your head."

"You can't literally see them."

She points at my skull. "Oh, I can. They whir quickly in that big brain of yours." She tilts her head. "What is it? What has put a sock in your brain power?"

I take a deep breath. "Jamison thinks I should talk to Kyle and tell him how I feel about Campbell. Basically, ask for his blessing or something."

I brace myself for her to say that's insane.

"Jamison is right," Roxy says, matter-of-factly.

"He is?"

"He's so right it's scary how right he is."

"Are you sure you're not saying this so you can regain the focus of your trivia partner?"

She shakes her head, her red hair whipping. "I'm saying it because some things in life are simple. We complicate them with worries, but at the end of the day, this is a simple thing. You tell your son how you feel, you make sure he's cool with it, and then you make your choice." She takes a sip of her iced tea then winks. "And I also really need a trivia partner with a laser focus."

I laugh, and when the hostess fires off the next question about the original name of the Beatles, I'm on that so damn fast it's no surprise we go on to win the whole round.

CHAPTER 27

Campbell

Miller's not alone when I find him at the brewery in the East Village, the one that houses retro arcade games too. He's jamming the joystick on a Frogger console, and by his side is a pretty brunette I recognize instantly.

I stride up to the two of them right as Miller's frog dies a brutal death.

"Ha! I win!" Ally says, thrusting a fist victoriously in the air. Bracelets jangle down her wrists, and her blue eyes twinkle.

He turns around and high-fives her. "Someday I will beat you."

I swear Miller holds her hand in that high five

longer than I've seen a high five last before.

His eyes find mine. He lets go and clears his throat. "Hey there."

Ally spins around and gives me a huge hug. "Campbell! Good to see you. Hope you don't mind I crashed your brotherly lunch date."

"Not at all. I haven't seen you in a while. How the hell are you? How's Chloe? How's work?"

Ally flashes a smile at the mention of her kid. "She's great. She's hanging out with my brother and Macy tonight. And work is crazy busy, but busy is good, so I can't complain. Good thing I can blow off steam taking this sorry bastard on in video games."

Miller bats his eyes at Ally. "You're going to help me though, right? You've been saying for years you can help improve my score in Frogger, Q*bert, and Donkey Kong. Ever since we met here."

"He thinks I can be his video game tutor," Ally says, rolling her eyes as if that's the height of hilarity.

"Hey. You're awesome at it. Plus, I need to be skilled at all things fun and games."

She pats him on the shoulder. "There, there. Poor Miller. It's sad when you haven't mastered all the fun in the universe, I know."

We head to a table, and after we order, I tip my chin at Ally, grateful I have the two of them for a double distraction today. "Did he tell you I've been trying to convince him to start singing with Rebecca Crimson?"

Ally straightens her spine. "You want him to sing with Rebecca?"

"Don't you think they'd sound fantastic?"

Ally stares at me, her expression blank. She says nothing.

Miller cuts in. "Then he said I should sing with you."

"And what did you say to that?" Ally's expression remains stoic.

Miller gives her a curious look. "I said you'd never sing with me anyway, since it would ruin our friendship. That was the correct answer, right?"

She seems to relax, but as she says yes, I wonder if that's not the right answer—if there's a deeper reason the two of them have never tried singing together. If there's more to the two of them in general.

But before I can marinate on the possibilities of my brother and his best friend, Ally smiles brightly at me. "Tell me what you've been up to. I want to know everything. Miller said you're doing great with the teaching, and there might be a new woman in your life."

Miller slaps a palm on the table. "Yes, your crush. What's the story?"

I heave a sigh then decide to serve up the details.

After I give them the basics, I swallow my pride and ask for advice. "What do I do next?"

Ally glances at Miller, smiling sheepishly. He smiles back at her but looks confused. "What's that for?" he asks her.

She's looking at him. "It's just so adorable. Don't you think that's adorable? Like, write-a-song-about-it adorable?"

Miller's eyes light up. "That would be a great tune."

I furrow my brow. "How is this helping me?"

They look away from each other and turn to me.

"Isn't it obvious?" she asks.

Miller rolls up his sleeves. "This is what you need to do."

I lean in and listen, and as they spell it out, I wonder if they're crazy or brilliant.

CHAPTER 28

Mackenzie

When Kyle comes home from practice that afternoon, my stomach is in knots, as twisted as my feelings are mixed up. It's not that he's some delicate little thing. It's just that I love him so damn much, and I want it all for both of us. I want the "lucky bitch" life.

He sets down his violin case and announces he's famished.

"Good thing I made one of my extra awesome sandwiches." I slide a plate over to him, and he tells me about his practice as he eats.

I listen. Once he's done, I'm ready for the floor. I've waited long enough, and it's not going to get any easier if I wait for him to finish the sandwich. I take a deep breath, meet his eyes, and speak from the heart. "Kyle, how would you feel if I wanted to date your music teacher?"

He tilts his head. "Campbell?"

"Yes." Worry crawls up my throat.

He scratches his jaw. "I thought you guys were already dating?"

I sputter. "You did?"

"Weren't you? You were always walking him to the door, and giving him sandwiches, and inviting him to stay for dinner. The way you two talked to each other made me think you were dating."

I have been busted by my son. My cheeks flush hot and red. "I like him. I like him a lot," I say.

He shrugs casually. "Then you should go out with him. Date him. Whatever adults call it these days."

Is it that simple? Evidently, it is to a thirteen-year-old. "I should?" I ask because I want to be certain.

He takes another bite, chewing thoughtfully before he sets down the sandwich. "I thought you already were, but maybe you stopped because you've been kind of sad."

And, yes, I am that transparent, so I give him total honesty. "I have been sad. I like him, but I was worried it would complicate things for you if I dated him. And you're sure it wouldn't bother you?"

He laughs lightly. "Mom, I don't care if you date him."

"But what if it doesn't work out?"

"We can do the lessons at Dad's house if you don't want to run into him. Or someone else can teach me. I'm fine with whatever you decide." He dives back into the sandwich, smiling as he finishes it. "Hey, did you hear the Yankees might be putting their first baseman on the trading block?"

"No, tell me more."

As I listen to the details of the newest trade speculation, I'm not sure why I'm so surprised Kyle's cool with this. I shouldn't be shocked. After all, I raised this kid to roll with the punches. I taught him how to handle whatever life throws at him. And he's doing exactly that. He's doing it admirably.

He's telling me life will throw him changes, and they might be for the best or they might suck, but whatever they are, he can handle them.

That makes me happy. Ridiculously happy.

When he clears his plate, he thanks me for making the sandwich. "And Mom?"

"Yes?"

"If it works out with Campbell, that would be great. If it doesn't work out, that would suck, but it would suck more for you than it would suck for me. And if it sucks for you, I will punch him and beat him up and basically make his life miserable. Does that sound reasonable?"

I laugh. "It sounds incredibly reasonable."

"Good." He snaps his fingers, as if he just remembered something. "I need to go to the music store. Can you come with me?"

"Of course," I say, thrilled that everything is business as usual with the person I love most.

CHAPTER 29

Campbell

When I return home that afternoon, I'm weighing Miller and Ally's suggestion. It's not a bad idea at all. But it's not the next step I need to take. Before I can do that, I need to talk to my daughter.

I find her in the kitchen, holding a plate of cookies. Ordinary chocolate chip cookies. *Uh-oh.* That means she's not baking for her show. She's baking for me.

"Dad." She sets down the cookies and points to a stool at the counter. "Sit down. We need to talk."

I privately groan in worry. Abject worry. "Is this when you tell me about a boy that you like?"

I've been dreading this moment my whole life.

"It's something like that."

I brace myself. I knew this would be coming soon. I give myself a pep talk as I cross to the counter. I'm ready. I can handle it. I can be a great dad and give her great advice on dudes.

Stay far, far away from them.

"What's going on? What's his name? Talk to me."

She stares at me. "His name is Campbell Evans."

I flinch in surprise. "What?"

"This conversation is about you." She rolls her eyes like the champ she is. "I know you like Mackenzie."

I start to speak, but she makes a shushing motion with her hand. "Don't speak. I have things to say right now."

I hold up my hands in surrender.

She slides the plate to me. "Take a cookie."

Refusing her is not an option, so I bite into one, and it's delicious.

"I know you like her a lot. It's kind of been obvious from day one. I can also tell you broke up with her."

I try to speak around the cookie.

Samantha shakes her head. "No. You need to listen right now, because I'm worried you're going to make a silly choice. And that's why I need to speak. I can tell the two of you split up. I can tell based on the fact that you're moping around. I'm a woman. I have intuition and I can sense these things. I know she likes you too."

I try to rein in a grin, but it's a futile effort.

"Listen, Dad. Here's the thing. Kyle and I have talked about this."

"You have?" I point to my chest. "Oh wait. Am I allowed to speak?"

"You're allowed one question. The *you have* question. Yes, we have spoken about it. We're very mature, and we know how to handle this."

"You do? Know how to handle this?"

She nods, looking solemn. "We want you to know if you were to get back together, you'd have our blessing."

I smile and laugh. "Are you serious? Because I was coming home to talk to you about this, Sam."

"You were?" She lets down her tough-girl guard.

"I was. You're right about everything. I've been moping, and I've been sad. I'm crazy for Mackenzie, but I wasn't sure if it was a bad idea to get involved with someone who's wrapped up in us already. Only, I've missed her so much, I wanted to talk to you about it."

"Dad, that's so sweet," she says, a grin stretching across her face. "I'm honored you wanted to ask. But it's your life, and I want you to be happy. This is the happiest you've been. And even though I don't remember Mom, I've never seen you care this much for a woman. I think it would be silly if you didn't take a chance with her."

A lump forms in my throat, and I swallow it. The almost-tears aren't for Sam's mom, and they're not even for Mackenzie. They're for this amazing girl of mine and how deeply she loves the people in her life.

She makes me realize I didn't do too bad at all raising her on my own. In fact, I've raised an incredible kid who's becoming a fantastic person. I tug her close and wrap my arms around her. "You turned out pretty great, do you know that?"

She rests her cheek against my shoulder. "That's because I have a great dad."

When we separate, she swipes her hand across her face. I run a hand down her hair. "I love you, Samantha."

"I love you, Dad," she says, then grins at me and punches my arm. "And stop worrying. Everything is going to be okay. The kid's all right, and so's the dad."

I smile wider than I ever have. "That is the best thing anyone's ever said to me."

"Okay, goofball. Let's go get your woman."

"Sounds like a plan."

"Also, the look on your face right now is priceless." She holds up her phone and snaps a picture then shows it to me. "This is the image of a guy who's falling in love."

I shake my head. "You're wrong, Sam. This is a guy who's already in love."

She points to the door. "Good. We have someplace to go, then."

CHAPTER 30

Mackenzie

"I thought the music store was two more blocks up Lexington?" I say when Kyle turns on Thirty-Sixth Street.

He shakes his head. "The one I like is down this street."

I shoot him a look like he's gone mad. "I'm not so sure. This block is full of restaurants and dry cleaners and—"

I stop when I realize what else is on this block.

A diner.

"Kyle? Are we actually going to a music store?"

His eyes twinkle. "What do you know? It's Willy

G's. I had no idea the music store was right next to the diner. And look who's there."

He points to the door and the two people standing in front of it: Campbell and his daughter.

Kyle smacks his forehead. "Oh, Mom, I remember where the store is. It's two more blocks up. See you later."

Kyle pivots and takes off, running to the corner. He's joined by his partner-in-parent-trapping as Sam bolts too, racing down the street and away from her dad.

"Whoa. Where are you guys going?" Campbell calls out in a loud, authoritative voice that's kind of weirdly hot.

Sam waves at him. "Don't worry. We're getting ice cream. Be right back."

They're gone. Just a couple of New York kids, making their way around the city.

I close the distance to Campbell, drinking up the sight of him in his jeans and pullover fleece, his stubble as sexy as it was the night I met him. His face is even more handsome, since I know the man behind the beautiful exterior.

I stop at the door, butterflies flapping inside me, hummingbirds beating their wings. "Hi."

The one-syllable word comes out breathy but full of meaning.

He greets me with a gorgeous smile that lights up the cloudy afternoon sky. "Hey, Sunshine."

I tip my forehead toward the kids, who clearly, no questions asked, plotted this get-together. I don't know who texted who first, and I don't know that it matters. "I think it's safe to say this is the official parent trap."

He grins. "Yeah, I think it is, and I couldn't be happier. I've been given an official blessing to ask you out on a date."

I laugh joyfully. So damn joyfully. "What do you know? I obtained my official blessing today too."

He reaches for my hand and links his fingers with mine, and we grin like happy clams. "Would you like to go on an official date with me to Willy G's? They have the best milkshakes and fries in all of New York City."

"I would love to."

He opens the door for me, and we head inside and grab a booth. We sit on the same side, and before we order, he cups my cheek and dusts a kiss across my lips. I shudder from that simple touch. "I'm looking forward to more of that."

He kisses me again. "Good. I have an endless supply for you."

We separate, and I can't stop looking at him, can't stop savoring this moment. "So we're dating. I like dating you."

"Actually," he says slowly, "there's something you need to know first."

I tense. Is there some other obstacle we have to overcome? Another reason we can't be together? "What is it?"

"We've already passed one of those milestones that happens when you date."

I relax, laughing. "You mean orgasms?"

"Not that, Sunshine. A different one. Because this is more than dating. This is being together." He runs the back of his fingers across my cheek, locking his eyes with mine. "I'm in love with you."

My heart soars out of my chest. "I'm in love with you too."

I lean closer and kiss his jaw, the corner of his mouth, his lips. I kiss him slowly, a torturous kind of kiss that makes him groan. He yanks me closer, whispering in my ear. "Now all I want to do is steal you away from here and take you."

I laugh and pull back. "I better be a good girl, then, since now might not be the best moment for that."

He slides his hand down my back, squeezing the top of my butt. "How about I buy the good girl I love a milkshake and fries?"

"Sounds like a reasonable consolation prize."

A little later, our kids show up, grabbing the bench across from us.

"Are you two finally together?" Sam asks in an exaggerated huff.

Campbell wraps his arm around me, squeezing my shoulder. "We're together."

"Took long enough," she says, pretending to be annoyed.

Kyle clears his throat. "It took *us* helping them along. What would they do without us, Sam?"

"They'd be so sad," she says with a frown.

"Thank God for us."

Samantha looks to her father. "Dad, do you think you should invite her to your show this week at The Grouchy Owl? Because I bet she'd love to go."

"I see the parent trap continues, and I think this is what it's going to be like dating you," I say to Campbell.

Sam laughs. "We're kind of a package deal."

Kyle chimes in, "Same here."

"You should just kiss," Sam says.

Campbell shakes his head. "I'm not kissing her in front of the two of you."

Kyle pretends to gag, and Sam laughs then holds up a hand and high-fives my son.

Somehow, that's all I need to decide it does make sense to lean closer to the guy I love and give him a quick kiss in front of our kids.

A chaste kiss.

Even so, it's all kinds of epic. Especially when the

four of us enjoy our afternoon snack together and then head to the movies.

It's a perfectly unexpected day.

EPILOGUE

Campbell

As I tune my guitar, Mackenzie aces another trivia question, nailing it when Big Ike herself asks which word goes before *vest*, *beans*, and *quartet*.

My woman looks to me and mouths *string* then bounces in her seat as she proceeds to write it on the paper in front of her. I'm willing to bet she'll rock every question tonight, and I'm right when her team is announced as the winner before our set begins.

I cheer for her, then she cheers for me when I turn on the mic and the guys and I launch into one of our fans' favorite tunes.

This time, the audience knows the song. We

aren't famous, but we have enough of a following that the crowd can sing along.

That's because The Grouchy Owl feels a little bit like home, and I like that. I like having a place where I can play, a place where I can be myself. I've missed performing, and this band has given me an outlet for that deep and longtime love of mine.

One song into the gig, Miller shows up, giving me a tip of the chin as he wanders in. I invited him, so I'm not surprised to see him.

What surprises me, though, is that Ally's here too.

I suppose I shouldn't be surprised. They're the best of friends, and they hang out all the time. But something looks different between the two of them now, and I don't know if it was that spark of jealousy I saw in her eyes at the brewery, or if I'm seeing in Miller a new awareness of the woman who's been his best friend for a long time.

As he heads to the bar with her, I put them out of my mind.

I'm much more interested in the woman who's dancing for me. The woman I'm going to take home tonight.

To *my* home.

Because my daughter is at a friend's house, and her son is with his father, and after I play this set, I get to play Mackenzie's body all night long.

In fact, it's time to let her know that.

Well, not in those precise words.

But when we finish the tune we're singing, I ask if the audience is ready for a new song.

"Do you take requests?" Mackenzie shouts with a goofy smile.

I meet her gaze, giving her a knowing grin. "I might. What do you want?"

"'Bring Him Home.'"

Cade scoffs from his spot onstage. "No way to *Les Mis*."

Mackenzie rattles off some pop tunes, since she's been shoring up her musical repertoire.

I shake my head to every request. "How about a new song I wrote?"

"Go for it," Miller shouts from the bar, and I nod at him.

"It was your idea," I tell him, since this is what Ally and Miller suggested I do at the brewery—write her a song.

"This is for a certain someone I like to call Sunshine."

Then I sing a brand-new number.

It's about falling in love unexpectedly. It's about taking chances. It's about realizing there's always going to be a reason to stay apart, but there are so many more reasons to be together.

When the song ends, I extend my hand, and tug

Mackenzie to the edge of the stage. I plant a huge kiss on her lips, one that says she's all mine and everyone can know it.

"I love your new song," she whispers.

"I love you."

* * *

Later that night, when we're alone in my home for the first time, I strip her down to nothing. I spread her out on my bed, savoring her body, kissing her everywhere. I make love to her, and it feels like the start of a fantastic new life together.

When we're through, she snuggles next to me and runs her fingers down my chest. "I'm going to make you pancakes in the morning."

I brush a kiss to her forehead. "I like that you like to feed me."

"I like to feed you, and I like to listen to music with you, and I like to watch *The Discovery Prism Show* with you. Most of all, I just like to hang out with you."

I bring her closer. "I think you're pretty epic."

"I think you're pretty epic too."

Then we watch an episode of our favorite show together. In bed.

It's so much better than watching it on the phone, because once the credits roll, I have her again.

One more time.

ANOTHER EPILOGUE

Mackenzie

My mouth is watering.

"How much longer?" I ask Samantha, doing my best to rein in the begging in my voice. But can anyone in the free world blame me? The cherry jam thumbprint cookies she's making for the Christmas party we're throwing tonight smell like heaven.

So do the ginger sandwich cookies with caramel buttercream filling. Not to mention the chocolate-covered peanut butter balls.

"They're almost ready," Samantha says, checking the timer on the oven.

"I'm dying, Sam. Dying, I tell ya," I say, swooning dramatically near the sink as if I'm going to faint in the kitchen.

"This is indeed torture of the highest degree," Ally says, chiming in from her spot at the counter next to Chloe, where they're sprinkling powdered sugar on top of the Nutella bread pudding. "You should try doing this without jamming your whole face into the bowl," Ally says.

"I think we should consider making a quick getaway with the bread pudding," Chloe suggests.

Samantha swivels around and points her whisk at Ally. "Do not ruin my Christmas treats. If you do, I will banish you from Samantha's Treat Zone."

Ally's blue eyes widen in apology. "No! Not the banishing!" She presses her hands together in a plea. "I promise not to stuff my face into the dessert."

As we work on finishing the baked goods, Ally starts humming. The pretty little tune is catchy, and it tickles my ear.

"Hey, Ally. What's that you're singing?"

"I like it. It's totes hummable," Sam says.

Ally doesn't answer right away. She simply smiles, a little impish and a little naughty.

"What's up your sleeve?"

She wiggles an eyebrow. "Well, you know how Miller finally decided to have auditions to find a new Garfunkel to his Simon?"

I nod, since Campbell filled me in on the basic details of Miller's plan. Campbell finally convinced his brother to take a brand-new direction in his singing career.

Ally sets down the powdered sugar, glances side to side as if to make sure no one is nearby, then beckons us both to come closer. We oblige, crowding near, eager for her to spill.

"Here's my plan."

Then she tells us, and the first words that come out of my mouth when she's done are, "That's genius."

Samantha squeals. "I can't wait to hear how it all goes down."

Later that night at the Christmas party, I steal a glance at Miller as he chats with Miles, who's in town during a break from his tour. Briefly, I wonder how Miller will react to Ally's plan.

Campbell comes up behind me to wrap his arms around me and brush his lips to my neck, and all my thoughts are for him.

I'm so lucky to be here, with the man I love and his family, who I also happen to adore.

No.

It's not luck.

I made this work. Just like I did with Kyle, and just like I did with my job. Seems this is the true pattern of my life.

"Hey, Campbell?" I whisper.

"Yeah?"

"You're a damn good track record."

He laughs lightly and kisses me more. "Sounds like the title of a good song."

Come to think of it, it does. The kind you want to sing not just all night, but all your life.

That's the kind of track record I know we're going to have.

THE END

Ready for more rock stars? Dying to know what Ally's plan is? Read all about it in the friends-to-lovers romance **Once Upon A Sure Thing available everywhere**! One-click now! If you liked Mackenzie and Campbell I think you'll fall in love with Ally and Miller! **Want more Mackenzie and Campbell? Sign up here to receive a bonus scene sent straight to your inbox!** https://www.subscribepage.com/RGT_bonus **If you've already signed up for my list, be sure to sign up again! It's the only way to receive the bonus scene, but rest assured you won't be double subscribed to the list! You can also sign up directly for my newsletter to receive an alert when these sexy new books are available at laurenblakely.com/newsletter including ONCE UPON A SURE THING!**

Another Epilogue

It's so easy being best friends with a gorgeous, talented, charming guy.

Said no woman ever. Except me.

My friendship with Miller is a sure thing — he's my plus one, my emergency contact, and my shoulder to lean on. He's also been by my side helping me raise one helluva awesome kid who's the center of my world.

Nothing will change our easy breezy friendship. Until I have the bright idea to convince him to start a new band with me.

Trouble is, our sizzling chemistry in the recording studio is getting harder to ignore, no matter how risky it might be.

***

Sing sexy songs with the woman you've been lusting after? Get up close and personal as you croon to the woman you've wanted for years?

Piece of cake.
NOT.

Performing with the sweet, sassy and insanely wonderful Ally is like one gigantic obstacle course of challenges for my libido. And my libido is one sexy love song away from kissing her senseless and taking her home.

But, I'm not a serious kind of guy, and she's not a one-night-stand kind of woman. **If we cross the horizontal line, we might risk our sure thing and end up out of tune forever...**

You can order ONCE UPON A SURE THING everywhere!

ACKNOWLEDGMENTS

It takes a village to publish a book and I am eminently grateful to Lauren Clarke, Jen McCoy, Helen Williams, Kim Bias, Virginia, Lynn, Karen, Tiffany, Janice, Stephanie and more for their eyes. Big thanks to Helen for the beautiful cover. Thank you to KP, Kelley, Keyanna and Candi. As always, my readers make everything possible.

ALSO BY LAUREN BLAKELY

FULL PACKAGE, the #1 New York Times Bestselling romantic comedy!

BIG ROCK, the hit New York Times Bestselling standalone romantic comedy!

MISTER O, also a New York Times Bestselling standalone romantic comedy!

WELL HUNG, a New York Times Bestselling standalone romantic comedy!

JOY RIDE, a USA Today Bestselling standalone romantic comedy!

HARD WOOD, a USA Today Bestselling standalone romantic comedy!

THE SEXY ONE, a New York Times Bestselling bestselling standalone romance!

THE HOT ONE, a USA Today Bestselling bestselling standalone romance!

THE KNOCKED UP PLAN, a multi-week USA Today and Amazon Charts Bestselling bestselling standalone romance!

MOST VALUABLE PLAYBOY, a sexy multi-week USA Today Bestselling sports romance, and MOST LIKELY TO SCORE, a sexy football romance!

THE V CARD, a USA Today Bestselling sinfully sexy romantic comedy!

WANDERLUST, a USA Today Bestselling contemporary romance!

COME AS YOU ARE, a Wall Street Journal and multi-week USA Today Bestselling contemporary romance!

PART-TIME LOVER, a multi-week USA Today Bestselling contemporary romance!

The New York Times and USA Today Bestselling Seductive Nights series including *Night After Night*, *After This Night*, and *One More Night*

And the two standalone romance novels in the Joy Delivered Duet, *Nights With Him* and Forbidden Nights, both New York Times and USA Today Bestsellers!

Sweet Sinful Nights, Sinful Desire, Sinful Longing and Sinful Love, the complete New York Times Bestselling high-heat romantic suspense series that spins off from Seductive Nights!

Playing With Her Heart, a USA Today bestseller, and a sexy Seductive Nights spin-off standalone! (Davis and Jill's romance)

21 Stolen Kisses, the USA Today Bestselling forbidden new adult romance!

Caught Up In Us, a New York Times and USA Today Bestseller! (Kat and Bryan's romance!)

Pretending He's Mine, a Barnes & Noble and iBooks Bestseller! (Reeve & Sutton's romance)

Trophy Husband, a New York Times and USA Today Bestseller! (Chris & McKenna's romance)

Far Too Tempting, the USA Today Bestselling standalone romance! (Matthew and Jane's romance)

Stars in Their Eyes, an iBooks bestseller! (William and Jess' romance)

My USA Today bestselling No Regrets series that includes
The Thrill of It (Meet Harley and Trey)
and its sequel
Every Second With You

My New York Times and USA Today Bestselling Fighting Fire series that includes
Burn For Me (Smith and Jamie's romance!)
Melt for Him (Megan and Becker's romance!)
and *Consumed by You* (Travis and Cara's romance!)

The Sapphire Affair series...
The Sapphire Affair
The Sapphire Heist

Out of Bounds
A New York Times Bestselling sexy sports romance

The Only One
A second chance love story!

Stud Finder

A sexy, flirty romance!

CONTACT

I love hearing from readers! You can find me on Twitter at LaurenBlakely3, Instagram at LaurenBlakelyBooks, Facebook at LaurenBlakelyBooks, or online at LaurenBlakely.com. You can also email me at laurenblakelybooks@gmail.com

Printed in Great Britain
by Amazon